"I'll be derned. Four toes."

A lot of intruders think they can slip onto my ranch without being detected. What they don't know is that a highly-trained cowdog can do a Snifferation Test and find all sorts of tracks.

And, bingo, after a thirty-second Snifferation, I found one. "Here we go, I've got him on radar! Look at this."

Drover squinted down at the track. "I'll be derned. Four toes."

"What? That's impossible. A Three-Toed Tree Sloth can't leave a four-toed track." I looked closer and studied the track. Hmmm. Four toes.

"And you know what? It kind of looks like...a porcupine track."

You know what? It did, and that sent my mind into a swirl.

A lot of your ordinary mutts would have quit the case right there. In other words, they would have fallen for the obvious....

the
Three-Toed Tree Sloth

John R. Erickson

Illustrations by Gerald L. Holmes

Maverick Books, Inc.

MAVERICK BOOKS, INC.
Published by Maverick Books, Inc.
P.O. Box 549, Perryton, TX 79070
Phone: 806.435.7611
www.hankthecowdog.com

First published in the United States of America by Maverick Books, Inc. 2018.

1 3 5 7 9 10 8 6 4 2

Copyright © John R. Erickson, 2018

All rights reserved

LIBRARY OF CONGRESS CONTROL NUMBER: 2018946894

978-1-59188-172-8 (paperback); 978-1-59188-272-5 (hardcover)

Hank the Cowdog® is a registered trademark of John R. Erickson.

Printed in the United States of America

To the memory of Carlos,
a good honest dog.

CONTENTS

CHAPTER ONE

The Mysterious Creature

It's me again, Hank the Cowdog. When I got the first intelligence reports about a Three-Toed Tree Sloth, I couldn't believe it. They're rare, exotic creatures that live in the jungles of South America, and no one had ever seen one in the Texas Panhandle. They eat trees and sometimes dogs too.

I was floored, shocked, and you will be too. I must warn you that this case is liable to get pretty scary before it gets any scarier. Does anyone feel brave enough to tag along? Use your own judgment.

Okay, let's get started. We'll take nothing but weapons and ammo for this mission.

You might recall that I run this ranch from my office on the twelfth floor of the Security Division's

1

Vast Office Complex. Looking out the huge windows, I can see ocean liners and tug boats in the harbor, and lines of traffic inching along on Broadway.

Great view. Most dogs don't get an office with such a view, but don't forget that I'm Head of Ranch Security. When a guy rises to a lofty position, he needs a lofty view of the world, right?

Well, I've got it. Sometimes I wonder if I really deserve it, but most of the time, heh heh, I'm pretty sure that I do.

The first report about the Tree Sloth came in around noon, as I recall. Yes, it was noon and I had already put in an eight-hour day, going over the crime reports that were stacked up on my desk.

It had been a quiet morning and I'd gotten a lot of work done, but then a stranger burst into my office and started yelling nonsense. "Hank, you'd better wake up!"

"Murgle honking the pork chop salad bowl."

"Pete just saw some kind of strange animal."

"Honk snerk...it was Beulah, and don't call her strange."

"It wasn't Beulah and you'd better wake up."

I opened my eyes and saw a smallish mutt with a stub tail. "Halt, stop in the name of the law! Who are you?"

"Well, I'm Drover, your best friend. Remember me?"

I narrowed my eyes and took a closer look. "Are you wearing a disguise? You look different now."

"Yeah, 'cause you were asleep."

"I was not asleep." I jacked myself up to a standing position and took a few faltering steps. "Drover, I must ask you a very important question. Where am I?"

"In our bedroom, under the gas tanks."

I glanced around at my surroundings. "Okay, this is starting to fit together. When you came in, did you see any pork chops?"

He giggled. "No, I think you were dreaming."

"Please don't giggle. I told you, I wasn't..." I took a deep breath of air. "All right, maybe I had dozed off. The work never ends around here, you know. What is the point of this intrusion?"

"Well, let me think." He rolled his eyes around. "Oh yeah. Pete saw some kind of strange creature."

"Strange creature? Why wasn't I informed? How can I run this ranch if nobody tells me about all the strange creatures running around?"

He let out a groan. "I tried but you were asleep. That's all you ever do."

I strolled over to him and looked deeply into his eyes. "Soldier, I'm going to forget you said

3

that. I know it's been a hard year, but you mustn't spread mustard about your commanding officer."

"You mean gossip?"

"Yes, exactly. That's what I said."

"No, you said mustard."

"That's absurd. Why would I have been talking about mustard?"

"I don't know, maybe you were dreaming about hamburgers."

"No, they were pork chops. There's been a mistake." I glanced around the office. "But let me remind you that we're in this thing together. A chain is only as strong as its winkest lick." He winked one eye and licked his chops. "Why did you do that?"

"Well, you said something about winks and licks, and all at once..."

"I said, 'weakest link.' We are a chain, Drover, and we're only as strong as our weakest link. Please try to remember that."

"Okay, I've got it."

"Good. Now, let's go see what kind of lies the cat is spreading around."

We turned out the lights and rode the elevator down to the ground floor, then went streaking away from the gas tanks and roared up to the

4

gravel drive behind the ranch house. There, I went to Total Lockdown on all four paws and slid to a sliding slop...*stop*, that is. I slid to a sliding slop beside the yard gate.

On the other side of the fence sat the cat. Mister Never Sweat. Pete.

Have we discussed my Position on Cats? I don't like 'em, never have. As a group, they're arrogant, lazy, and prone to sneaky behavior, and Pete is worse than most. I rarely do business with cats, but sometimes it can't be avoided. This appeared to be one of those situations.

The little pest was licking his front paw with long strokes of his tongue. He looked up and gave me his usual smirk. "My, my, it's Hankie the Wonderdog! What brings you to my little corner of the world?"

I swaggered over to him. "Never mind the small talk, Kitty. I'm on a tight schedule."

His eyes grew wide. "Really!"

"That's correct. Drover said you turned in a report."

"Did I? I wonder what it could have been."

My lips twitched into a snarl. "Hurry up, Pete. I know you love wasting my time but this isn't the day for it."

He fluttered his eyes and grinned. "Oh, you

5

mean the strange animal?"

"Drover said it was a strange *creature*, not just an animal. Tell me about the so-called strange creature."

"Oh, that! Well, yes, I saw one."

"Go on and stick with the facts."

"Well, Hankie, with my own eyes, I saw..." He leaned toward me and lowered his voice. "...a Three-Toed Tree Sloth."

"That's rubbish. Toads don't live in trees."

He heaved a sigh. "Not a toad, Hankie. It's a creature that has three toes and lives in trees. It's called a sloth, a Three-Toed Tree Sloth. I'll bet you can't say it."

I laughed in his face. "Oh yeah? Check this out. Free-Toed Tree Toad."

"That's wrong, Hankie. Three. Toed. Tree. Sloth."

"Pete, if I can't pronounce it, I don't believe in it."

He shrugged. "Well, I guess you're not interested."

"I guess I'm not." I whirled away from the little crook. "Come on, Drover, this cat is wasting our time."

As we marched away, I heard Pete's voice behind me. "Maybe you don't care that he's eating trees."

A buzz of electricity leaped down my spine. I stopped in my tracks, whirled around, and marched back to the fence. There, I beamed the cat an icy glare. "He was doing *what*? Did you say the creature was eating my trees? Without permission?"

"Um hm, that's what Tree Sloths do, Hankie. They eat trees, chew them right down to the ground. But I'm sure you already knew that."

"Of course I did. If you knew it, I knew it, only I knew it first. Don't forget who's Head of Ranch

Security." I moved closer and lowered my voice. "Maybe it was a beaver, Pete. Beavers eat trees, you know."

The cat shook his head. "It wasn't a beaver, Hankie. Beavers live in the water. Sloths climb trees. I saw him up in a tree."

I paced a few steps away and tried to sort things out. Did I dare trust the testimony of a cat? Cats are notorious for spreading lies and causing trouble, and they do it just for sport. They don't have jobs, you know, and when time begins to drag, they plot mischief. It's just the nature of a cat.

But what bothered me most was that...how can I say this? What bothered me most was that I had never heard of a Tree-Toed Slip Slop, and I sure didn't want Kitty to know what I didn't know.

Before I exchanged another word with the little scrounge, I needed to gather some more information about this mysterious creature, before something really bad happened to our ranch trees.

CHAPTER TWO

Barn Robbers

We call it "research," gathering background information for a case we have under investigation, and it's a very important part of my work with the Security Division. See, a lot of dogs won't take the time to do a proper job of researching a case, because...well, let's face it. It's too much trouble. It's hard work. Ordinary mutts would rather chew a bone, snap at flies, or sleep.

Show me a dog that sleeps his life away and I'll show you a mutt that never solves a case.

Anyway, where were we? Oh yes, I had just finished an interrogation of the local cat and had managed to extract an incredible pack of lies and half-truths about a mysterious creature called the Hammer-Toed Slip Slop.

Wait. It was called Three-Footed Toad Frog.

I don't care what Pete called it, but he claimed that it had devoured and destroyed three hundred trees on my ranch.

It was called the Three-Toed Tree Sloth. There we go.

But regardless of what we called the thing, I was pretty sure it was nothing but a pack of lies, because...well, the story came from a cat, and cats would rather spin lies than eat ice cream. They are notorious twisters of the truth, and we never build a case around the testimony of a cat. Never.

On the other hand, it was a pretty disturbing pack of lies, and a dog in my position must remain open to the possibility that, once in a great while, a cat will mess up and tell the truth. In other words, I had to do some more digging on the case, and that brings us back to that word we discussed before, "research." I had to do my research on this deal.

I left Drover with the cat, which tells you a lot about Drover. He was so bored with his own little life, he had nothing better to do than hang out with a cat, but let's don't get started on that.

I hiked up the hill to the machine shed, doing Visual Sweeps for any sign of a mysterious creature. The VS turned up no leads, but then I began picking up signals of an unauthorized vehicle that was approaching headquarters from the north. It was moving at a low rate of speed, creeping along, and that seemed pretty suspicious.

Was it possible that the Tree Sloth was driving around the ranch in a vehicle? Probably not. Any creature that eats trees can't drive a pickup, so skip that. This appeared to be something entirely new and unrelated to Pete's phony report.

I came to a stop, lifted Earoscanners, and began pulling in Earatory Data. It confirmed my original impression: there was something not right about this deal. I dove into a clump of ragweeds...wait, is "dove" the right word?

Dive, dove, diven. Diven.

I diven into some ragweeds and went undercover. There, peeking through the weeds, ACHOO! I sneezed. This was the fall of the year, don't you see, and we'd had enough rain over the summer to produce a huge crop of ragweeds, I mean, they were tall and thick and everywhere.

ACHOO!

And one of the things you might not know about ragweeds is that they are Sneezaromic Plants, which means ACHOO they release high levels of ACHOO that cause people and dogs to go into fits of ACHOO! See what I mean?

ACHOO!

This was pointless, trying to do a Stake Out of an unidentified creeping vehicle, while sneezing my fool head off. I leaped out of the stupid weeds and took up a position right in the middle of the road. If the trespassers planned to break into the machine shed and steal tools, they would have to deal with me first.

Oops. I allowed my suspicion to slip out, so we might as well go public with it. See, I had a strong suspicion that whosomever was inside that pickup might be working for Midnight Supply. You've never heard of Midnight Supply, right? Well, it's a secret code word we use in the Security Business, so let me explain.

Midnight Supply is code for crooks, thieves, and bad guys who steal tools. They case out a location during the daylight hours, don't you see, then come back after dark and rob things.

Midnight Supply. It's a pretty clever way of putting it, isn't it? And you know what? I invented it myself. No kidding. I get a kick out of experimenting with language and inventing new terms.

Now...where were we? Hmm. Okay, language. Language is very important to anyone who isn't an ignoramus. Wait. Thieves in a pickup.

The pickup was still coming at that same creepy speed, I mean, the driver obviously had some kind of mischief on his mind. He was now approximately a hundred and fifty feet away and closing. It was time for me to move beyond our Hide In The Weeds procedure.

I hit Sirens and Lights, and cut loose with three crisp Warning Barks: "Halt! Stop! This is a Secured Area and we'll need to see some ID!"

The vehicle kept coming. Okay, this would require sterner measures. I spread my legs apart, took a firm grip on the earth below, and fired off three more Big Ones.

"Pull over and get out, hands over your heads, move it!"

I wouldn't have been surprised if the jerks had sped up and tried to run me over. They do that sometimes, and blow their horn and hang out the window and yell insults as they go roaring past. The mailman is one of the world's worst, and on several occasions, he has even spit tobacco juice at me.

I'm not kidding. The guy has no respect for authority. None.

But all at once, this crisis took a surprising turn. You won't believe this. Neither did I. The

13

pickup actually came to a sudden stop, and we're talking about Full Brakes and sliding on the gravel. Both doors flew open and two male suspects leaped out of the vehicle, and get this: They came out with HANDS UP!

Do we have time for a description of the bad guys? I guess so. The one on the passenger-side was kind of stocky in the shoulders. The driver was tall and skinny. Both wore jeans, faded shirts, baseball caps, and lace-up boots, and those were important clues.

Do you see the meaning? They weren't cowboys! Cowboys wear cowboy clothes. These guys were dressed like…I don't know, like farmers or welders or robbers. Yes, they wore the standard uniform of barn robbers.

Okay, at that point, it got very interesting. When they got out of the pickup, you'll never guess what happened next, so pay attention. They were really scared and had their hands high in the air, and the skinny one said, "Don't shoot, officer, we're just tourists from Dallas!"

Tourists from Dallas?

"We heard there's a world-famous guard dog on this ranch."

A world-famous…what was going on here?

"They call him Hank the Cowdog. Have you

seen him around?"

What? Hey, that was ME!

"He's known all over the world, even in Dallas."

No kidding? Wow, did you hear that? I had no idea...hey, those guys weren't barn robbers. They were just a couple of tourists from Big D, and they had come to meet...well, ME, what else can you say?

I was overwhelmed. I mean, Dallas is a huge, important city, and it's a long way from the Panhandle. These two fine gentlemen had driven six or seven hours just to...all at once, a wave of humility washed over me, and I must admit that in my long and colorful career, waves of humility had seldom washed over me, but this time...well, I was speechless.

I shut off Sirens and Lights, and lowered the strip of hair that had risen up along my backbone. Holding my head at a dignified angle, I marched toward them. After making such a long drive, they deserved...

Huh?

I heard the sounds of laughter, the kind of rude, irreverent snorting you'd expect from... never mind, we'll skip the rest of this.

Look, I'm a very busy dog and don't have time

for nonsense. I mean, somebody on this ranch has to WORK once in a while.

You know, they're always complaining about how hard it is to make a living in the ranching business, battling drought and blizzards and the cattle market, but oh how different things might be if they stopped pulling childish pranks on their dogs and DID A DAY'S WORK.

It's shocking, all the things I have to put up with around here, and we're talking about every day. They think they're so funny, but they're not. They're nothing but a couple of goof-offs, in the same class as the mailman, only twice as bad, and I refuse to say one more word about it.

Don't beg, I'm not going to talk about it.

Oh well, you've probably figured it out anyway. We might as well get it over with.

Those "tourists from Dallas" turned out to be my so-called friends, Slim and Loper, the so-called cowboys on this ranch. They'd spent the morning planting wheat, which is one of the routine chores on this ranch in the fall. They plant wheat in the ground, in hopes that it will sprout wheat plants and make winter pasture for the cattle.

That's why they weren't wearing their cowboy clothes. When they do the farming (which they don't enjoy), they wear regular work clothes, and

any dog would have missed that clue.

Hey, when they wear different clothes, how are we supposed to know who they are? And why were they creeping along in the pickup? Your top of the line cowdogs notice every tony dovetail...every tiny detail, I mean, and when we see a vehicle that creeps along, we naturally assume that the people inside are creeps.

It's simple, mathematical, and scientific. Creeping = Creeps = barn robbers. I can't make it any plainer than that. The fact that it turned out to be wrong doesn't mean it wasn't scientific.

It really burns me up when they hatch these pranks and make a mockery of my work, and one of these days...phooey.

CHAPTER THREE

The Whistling Rooster Blues

Well, they had their little fun, making me look silly, and oh how they enjoyed it! They roared with laughter, doubled over, and slapped their thighs. Slim even slapped his hand on the hood of the pickup. And of course I had to endure their smart remarks.

Loper: "Did we fool you, Hankie?"

No.

Slim: "Thanks for holding your fire, pooch."

Was that supposed to be funny? Pathetic.

They climbed back into the pickup and drove on to the machine shed. I was kind of disappointed they didn't offer me a ride in the cab. That would have given me the opportunity to *turn them down* and give them my Snub of the Year: "Me, ride in

19

the same vehicle with a couple of clowns? No thanks, I have a reputation to protect. I'll walk, and enjoy every second of it."

I didn't get the chance to blow them away with a cutting refusal to be seen riding around with them, but I did manage to salvage one little piece of revenge. I didn't give them Escort to the barn.

See, under Normal Ranch Protocol, dogs take the lead position and do Escort for every vehicle that enters ranch headquarters. We clear out the chickens and cats, and lead the vehicle to an Authorized Parking Space. It's part of the Security Division's Regular Service Package, and THEY DIDN'T GET IT.

I walked to the barn by myself, took my sweet time, and made no effort to contribute to their safety or comfort. They had to find their own way and their own parking space. So there!

By the time I got there...did I mention that I took my sweet time? I did, and we're talking about making a big deal out of how much *I didn't give a rip* about them or anything they were doing. I just didn't care.

By the time I reached the barn, they had backed up to the big sliding doors and were loading fifty-pound sacks of something into the bed of the pickup. What was that stuff? Oh yes, seed wheat. Wheat seed. In the field, they would pour the seed into a metal bin on the "Dempster drill," the piece of equipment they used for planting wheat.

See, when you plant wheat, you put *wheat* seed into the bin. If you put oat seed into the bin, you would be planting...maybe this is obvious, but what's not so obvious is why they called that piece of equipment a "drill."

Why would they call it a drill? I had no idea. A drill turns in circles and makes a hole.

Nobody on this outfit wants to hear what the dogs think, but I have an opinion on this. A device that plants wheat should be called a "planter." No dog would call it a drill, but they called it a drill anyway, and didn't care what I thought about it.

I don't mean to rave, but it gives you an idea of what we have to put up with on this outfit.

Anyway, they were loading sacks of wheat seed into the back of the pickup. I didn't offer to help and had to sit there, listening to them blow like the wind.

Slim: "I'm sure glad Uncle Bert ain't around to see me today."

Loper: "Who's Uncle Bert?"

"Well, he was a cowboy. He worked on ranches between Seminole and Roswell. He made his

21

living with a horse and a rope."

"Here we go again." Loper sighed.

Slim kept on, "Back in the old days, when a man hired onto a ranch as a *cowboy*, he spent his days ahorseback."

"This fall weather sure has been nice."

"No ranch boss would have stuck a top hand on a flea-bag diesel tractor, driving around in circles from daylight to dark. It would have started a cowboy rebellion."

"Sally May's birthday is coming up next week."

Slim pitched his sack into the pickup. "Your hearing aid needs a new battery."

"I save it for things that are worth hearing."

"Well, you need to hear this. Our horses haven't been rode in so long, they don't even remember our names. If you ever show up in the saddle lot again, old Dunny might think you're Jesse James."

Loper walked back into the barn. "La la la la."

Slim followed. "And he might bite your nose off. It would improve your looks, but it's sad when the world falls into such a sorry state."

"La la la la."

"And by the way, that tractor I'm driving puts out a constant spray of diesel fuel."

They emerged from the barn, each lugging a sack of seed. Loper said, "Maybe it's got a leak in the fuel line."

"Well, of course it's got a leak! When I get home at night, I smell like I was baptized in diesel. Even the skunks run when they see me coming."

"Maybe you ought to take a bath once in a while."

"Loper, I'm scared to run the hot water heater, 'cause the pilot light might set off the diesel fumes and blow me up."

Loper chuckled, shook his head, and looked up at the sky. "Here's an idea. We'll sell the horses and auction off the saddles and use the money to buy you a new tractor. Then you can drive it around the ranch, twelve months out of the year, and maybe you'll quit whining."

Slim stared at him. "Loper, you ain't funny."

"We'll fix the fuel leak when we get the wheat in the ground."

They went back into the barn for more sacks, and they were still growling at each other. To be honest, I was finding their conversation a little tiresome. I mean, they go on like this all the time and nothing ever changes.

Next week, the tractor would still be leaking fuel and they would still be arguing about it. I know these guys.

I took a big stretch and yawn, and started back to the office. I'd been up for hours, doing

Traffic and Patrols, and a short nap might fit right into my plans. But then I caught sight of something out of the corner of my eye, and it caused me to make a sudden turn to the left.

I saw someone in the distance and didn't want to get trapped into a conversation with him. Can you guess who it might have been? Here are a few hints: he walked upright on two legs, wore feathers, and whistled his words when he talked, which was most of the time.

J.T. Cluck, the Head Rooster.

I ducked my head and hurried away, hoping he wouldn't see me, but of course he did.

"Hey, pooch, hold up! We need to talk." Groan. I stopped and here he came. "Where do you think you're going in such an all-fired rush?"

"I have a ranch to run. I'm a very busy dog."

"Well, too bad. We've got things to talk about."

I heaved a sigh. "I'll give you five minutes."

He glanced over both shoulders and leaned toward me. "Pooch, we've got problems in the chicken house."

"Oh?"

"Yes sir, but I don't want it blabbed all over the ranch."

"I don't blab. What's the problem?"

"You ever had mites?"

24

"Never heard of 'em. What are mites?"

"Little bitty bugs. Chickens get 'em and they cause a terrible itch. Elsa thinks one of our hens has mites, 'cause she scratches all the time."

"Tell her to quit scratching."

"You ever tried to tell a woman to quit scratching?"

"No."

"Well sir, I tried to talk to her about it and it turned into a wreck. She cried for thirty minutes. I couldn't get a word in edgewise, and then she went right on scratching."

"Then let her scratch."

"It ain't that simple. She scratches all night long, is the problem. She scratches in her sleep and wakes up everybody else. I'm living in a henhouse with nineteen women who can't sleep, and one who sleeps but can't quit scratching. Pooch, this is becoming a crisis."

I shouldn't have laughed, but what can you do? I laughed. "J.T., I don't mean to sound cruel…"

"Then quit laughing!"

"…but this is your problem, not mine."

I tried to leave but he followed me. "Listen, dog, what happens if word leaks out that we've got bugs in the chicken house? It would cause a scandal, is what it would do."

I stopped and studied him for a moment. "J.T., there's something I'm curious about."

"Well, good. Maybe there's still hope for you."

"J.T., when you talk, you whistle your words."

He flinched. "That's right, mister. Are you making fun?"

"No, I'm just curious. See, I've known quite a

few chickens in my time and you're the only one who talks with a whistle. What's the deal?"

He was silent for a long time, gazing off into the distance. "I'll tell you the whole story, pooch, but you can't be blabbing it around."

"I told you, I don't blab."

"Good, 'cause it's kind of mysterious how it all come about. I put the whole story into a song."

"A song? You wrote a song?"

"That's right. You want to hear it or not?"

"Actually..."

"Good. Here goes."

Well, I had walked into this mess and it appeared that I would have to listen to it.

The Whistling Rooster Blues

One day when I was younger, me and ma
    was on a walk.
She said, "J.T.,you're almost grown and
    we need to have a talk."
I said, "Okay, I'm ready to listen to
    whatever is on your mind."
She said, "The world is big and wide, my
    boy, and here is what you'll find...

"Son, I want to break this to you easy. In

this life, you can squawk or cluck, but
   you'll never be able to whistle."

I must admit that I was shocked. I had
   never given a thought
To whether I could whistle or whether I
   could not.
It made me kind of curious, I wondered
   what she meant.
"Who says that I can't whistle? Is it
   wrote down in cement?"

She said, "Anyone who whistles, whistles
   through his teeth. And son, you ain't got
   any.   You're a chicken, a rooster."

Well, maybe I was a rebel and had a chip
   on my shoulder,
'Cause what she said just made me mad
   and I began feeling bolder.
I was determined to prove her wrong and
   took off like a missile.
For forty days and forty nights, I worked
   on my whistle.

Well, I graduated from Music School and
   whistled her a tune,

She was just astounded, I mean, it knocked
her to the moon.
She said, "How did you do that? It strains
my disbelief.
There's no way that a rooster can whistle
without teeth!"

I said, "Hey Ma, did you notice that I even
whistle when I talk?" She said, "Yes, I did,
and you sound ignert!" Huh. Didn't
expect that.

I've got the Whistling Rooster Blues, the
Whistling Rooster Blues.
Sometimes what you wish for you wish that
you could lose.
Now I've got a genuine handicap and
whistle on every word,
And my very own momma thinks I sound
absurd.

And that's how I become the world's first
whistling rooster. Got them Whistling
Rooster Blues.

He finished the song and stared down his beak
at me. "Well, there it is, that's the whole story and

it's true, every word of it. What do you think?"

"It's not a bad little song."

"It's a great song, best I ever wrote."

"And I agree with your mother."

"Huh? What do you mean by that?"

"When you whistle your words, you sound ridiculous. Now, if you'll excuse me, I have a ranch to run."

I walked away and left him to bore himself.

CHAPTER FOUR

Elsa's Frightening Report

W here were we? Oh yes, I had just endured a painful musical experience, listening to a rooster croak a silly song about his whistling handicap, and I turned to leave.

J.T. called out, "Hey, what about the bugs?"

"I don't care about your bugs or your scandals."

Again, he stepped into my path, his weird red eyes blazing. "All right, Mister Hot Shot Guard Dog, then let's get down to another problem, and this one's really serious."

"I'll give you two minutes."

He glanced around and lowered his voice. "Last night, that old hen was scratching like crazy and Elsa couldn't sleep. She went out for a walk."

"Hurry up."

"I'm a-getting there, just hold your horses. Elsa went for a little stroll in the moonlight, see, and suddenly and all at once, she seen..." He had my attention and I waited to hear the rest of his report, but what came out was a ridiculous little chicken burp. "That dad-ratted heartburn's got me again!"

My spirits sank. "Oh brother! Is this going to turn into another of your heartburn stories?"

"Well, no, but I ate a squash bug this morning and now he's tearing me up." He squeezed out another ridiculous burp. "You know, squash bugs look pretty appetizing at first, but what a guy forgets is that they release that smell. You ever smelled a squash bug?"

"Do I look dumb enough to go around smelling bugs?"

"Pooch, we do it all the time."

"Exactly my point. Hurry up."

"Well, when you get squash bugs stirred up, they release this smell, and it's kind of sickly sweet. When the bug gets down to your gizzard, the sweet is gone and what's left is the sickly. It'll give you the darndest heartburn you ever saw."

I moved closer and exposed two rows of fangs. "J.T., try to concentrate."

"That's what I'm a-doing."

"No more heartburn stories. Did Elsa see

something in the dark or not?"

"She sure did, but how'd you know?"

"You were fixing to tell me about it when you got overwhelmed by your heartburn."

"Oh yeah, it's a-coming back to me now. I'll finish the story, if you'll quit butting into my business."

"Hurry up. Two minutes and I'm gone."

He hiked up one leg and a tucked it under his wing. Roosters stand that way sometimes, I don't know why. Maybe it helped him focus his tiny mind.

"Elsa was out walking, don't you know, and all at once, she seen some kind of..." His voice dropped into a whispered horse...into a hoarse whisper, that is, and he said, "She seen some kind of strange creature in the dark!"

A strange creature in the dark. He had my full attention now. "J.T., before we go any farther, I must know if you've discussed this matter with the local cat."

"The local what?"

"Cat. His name's Pete, otherwise known as Mister Never Sweat. He stays in the yard."

"Oh, him. No, I don't talk to cats. You can't trust 'em, 'cause you never know what's going on behind them eyes. They've got weird eyes."

"I agree. Go on with your story and get straight to the point. What kind of strange creature did Elsa see? I need facts and details."

I detected a hint of fear in his eyes. "Pooch, Elsa had never seen anything like this in all her put-together years."

"Description."

"Huh?"

"I need some kind of description."

"Oh." His gaze lifted to the sky. "Cranes are flying south."

"You mean it was a bird?"

"Yes, they're birds, long skinny legs and a long beak. They eat fish."

"Elsa saw a bird eating fish in the middle of the night?"

His eyes drifted down to me. "What are you talking about?"

"What are YOU talking about?"

"I said the cranes are flying south." He pointed a wing toward a V-shaped formation of birds in the sky. "They do it every year in the fall. Can't you hear 'em honking?"

"I hear them honking and I don't care about cranes. What did Elsa see in the dark?"

"Oh yeah. Well, let me think. She said..."

This next part was strange. He'd been

standing on one leg, remember? And all at once he started using the three toes on his uplifted leg to scratch his wingpit...armpit, whatever you call that thing on a...

Wait, hold everything! A Three-Toed Tree Toad has three toes, and so does a chicken's foot. Was this some kind of clue that I'd been missing? Notice that in both examples, we have a common theme: THREE TOES.

I leaned closer and listened, memorizing every tiny detail. J.T. was scratching himself and said, "That old biddy gave me her bugs! I knew this was going to happen!"

Forget the three toes on a chicken's foot. It wasn't a clue and I was one breath away from blowing up, but had to muster the patience to drag some facts out of the witness.

"J.T., stop scratching and finish the story. Think. Concentrate. What kind of creature did Elsa see in the dark?"

He stopped scratching and stared at several feathers floating around in the air. "Well, here's what she told me, pooch, and these were her very words. She said this strange creature looked like a beaver with a bad haircut."

Those words sent a shock wave down my back. "A beaver with a bad haircut?"

"That's what she said. It wasn't exactly a beaver, and it had a crazy hairdo."

I began pacing in front of him, as I often do when a case is coming together. "J.T., I've been working this case for weeks and I think we're finally onto something. Question." I stopped and whirled around. "Is it possible that she saw a Three-Footed Tree Sloth?"

"Never heard of it."

"That wasn't the question. This court doesn't care whether you've heard of it or not. The question was, could it have been a Slew-Footed Tree Sloth?"

"Well..."

"Yes or no?"

"You're too pushy."

"Yes or no?"

"Well, it could have been anything, so...yes."

"Bingo! Last question. Was this creature eating trees?"

"Huh? Trees? No, she seen him in front of the barn, there wasn't any trees."

"Perfect! Just as I suspected. He wasn't eating trees, which proves that he was *looking* for trees to eat." I marched over to him and laid a paw upon his shoulder. "We've blown this case wide open, and I'll see that you get a little badge for this."

"A what?"

"A badge. We'll make you an Honorary Agent of the Security Division."

"Well, hoop-tee-doo." He patted his chest and let out another little chicken-burp. "I'd rather have a teaspoon of baking soda. That squash bug is burning me up."

I left him there, boiling in his own gastric juices and muttering about squash bugs. What a birdbrain. He had almost bored me into a coma, but I had managed to wring some very important information out of him.

Let me go over it again, just to make sure you're up to speed. I now had a second eyewitness account, claiming that ranch headquarters had been penetrated by some shadowy, dreaded, mysterious creature. In other words, I had to face the possibility that there might have been a speck of truth in Pete's pack-of-lies story.

That was good news and bad news. First, the case was really coming together, but second, I would have to go back to the yard and do business with the cat, and the very thought of it made me ill. You already know my Position on Cats, so I won't repeat that I don't like Sally May's rotten little cat and absolutely hate doing business with him. But it had to be done.

Why? To protect our trees. Trees are scarce in the Texas Panhandle, but we've got some nice ones on my ranch: cottonwoods, native elms, hackberries, and chinaberries.

And guess who's in charge of protecting them. Me, the Head of Ranch Security.

I'm pretty fussy about who uses my trees and what they do with them. Take birds as an example. During the summer months, we've got a million noisy unemployed birds on this ranch, and I spend half my time barking them away from my trees.

Turn your back on birds for half an hour and they'll take over. They never ask permission and they seem to think the trees belong to *them*. Well, they don't. Those are MY trees and uninvited birds aren't welcome.

And neither are creatures that eat them, such as your Toad-Footed Tree Slippers. I'd never seen one with my own eyes, but if they ate trees, we were going to have problems. I hated to build a case on the testimony of a rooster and a cat, but those were the cards Life had dealt me.

In other words, I had to find out what else Pete knew about the creature. If that meant being nice to the little snot...well, it had to be done.

I found him with Drover near the yard gate, just where I had left them. I walked into the path of Kitty's scheming yellow gaze. He smirked and said, "Well, well! You're back."

"I'm back, but it has nothing to do with you."

He fluttered his eyelids. "Then I wonder what it could be."

"That's none of your business, but if you must know, I'm here to speak to Drover." I turned to the runt. "You need to find something else to do with your life. Why don't you go get a drink?"

"Well, I'm not thirsty."

"Go eat some dog food."

"It hurts my teeth."

"Then take a hike, get some exercise."

"Well, this old leg's been acting up."

"Drover, when you spend hours and hours talking to the cat, it reflects badly on all of us in the Security Division. Go find something else to do."

"Yeah, but..."

"Scram! Buzz off.

He hung his head and went slinking away. "You don't need to screech. I hate being yelled at in the morning."

When he was gone, I turned back to the cat. I was ready to give him the interrogation of his life.

CHAPTER FIVE

The Funnel
of Logic

Are you still with me? Good, because I had Pete the Barncat in the witness stand and was fixing to rip his testimony apart, bit by bit.

He was staring at me and said, "You're back and it has nothing to do with me, but here we are, alone. I'm wondering what it means."

I turned away from him and tried to collect my thoughts. "Pete, let me begin by saying that I would rather be anywhere else but here."

"And?"

"Doing business with you is very painful."

"Poor doggie!"

"And it doesn't help when you say, 'Poor doggie.'"

"What's the business, Hankie?"

This was going to be a difficult interrogation.

First, he had something I needed and he knew it. Second, cats love to waste time. They don't have anything to do and they're experts at loafing. Third, Pete was dumber than a box of rocks. I hate to put it that way, but it's the truth.

Hencely, getting information out of Pete is always an ordeal, but it had to be done. I began pacing back and forth in front of him, as I often do when my mind has shifted into a higher level of performance.

"Pete, I need your help on this case."

Silence. Then, "Oh really? Which case would that be?"

"The Toad-Footed Tree Slipper."

"Oh that case! Yes, the Three-Toed Tree Sloth. It's hard to say, isn't it?"

"No. Okay, it's hard to say, but here's the point: I need to nail down the facts. One of our hens turned in a report. She saw a strange creature walking around ranch headquarters."

He stared at me for a moment, and a smirk twitched at his mouth. "Did she! My, how exciting."

"Skip the dramatics. Tell me more."

As you might expect, he took his sweet time in answering. It was typical cat behavior. If we say hurry up, they slow down. If we say slow down, they slow down even more.

He rolled his eyes up to the sky and flicked the end of his tail back and forth. "Well, let me think, Hankie. It must have been this morning. Or was it yesterday?"

"Quit stalling."

"It was this morning, Hankie. I was sitting in the iris patch."

"Loafing, I'm sure. Go on."

"I was sitting in the iris patch and heard a sound coming from those trees."

"Which trees? Be precise."

He pointed a paw toward a line of trees north of the house, which we often refer to as the "shelter belt." It's a belt of trees, don't you see, that shelters the house from cold winter winds, which is why we call it...

Maybe this is obvious.

He pointed toward the shelter belt, the cat did, and continued talking in his nerve-grating voice. "I climbed over the fence and went to investigate, Hankie, and that's when I saw..." He dropped his voice to a spooky whisper. "...the creature!"

"Okay, you saw a creature, a strange animal. What made you think it was a...whatever you called it."

"A Three-Toed Tree Sloth."

"That's correct. Go on."

"Well, Hankie, he had three toes and was eating our precious trees."

I stopped pacing and whirled around to face the cat. "Hold it right there. Already I've found a hole in your story."

"Oh really?"

"Yes. Check this out. If the creature had four feet, how could it have only three toes? You're one toe short, Kitty. Your math is totally messed up. What happened to that other toe?"

He heaved a sigh and rolled his eyes toward the sky. "Three toes on each foot, Hankie."

I stuck my nose in his face. "Oh yeah? Then try this on for size. Four feet multiplied by three toes equals fourteen toes."

"Twelve toes, Hankie."

"That's what I said, twelve toes. If he's got twelve toes, why are you calling him a Three-Toed Tree Chopper, huh? What are you hiding?"

The cat drummed his claws on the ground. "Hankie, if you want to change the name to Twelve-Toed Tree Sloth, that's fine with me. Whatever makes you happy."

Was this some kind of trick? Maybe not.

"Never mind. We'll stick with the original name, but you should remember that I'm checking every little detail of your clackulations."

"Calculations, Hankie. Shall we continue?"

"We'll continue when I'm ready to continue." I began pacing again. "Let's continue. Before I commit troops to this deal, I need to know more about the enemy. How tough is he? What's his fighting style? Does he eat dogs?"

"Oh no, Hankie, not at all. Sloths are slothful."

"What does that mean?"

"They're docile."

I marched over to him and glared down into his face. "You're using big words and that really annoys me."

"But Hankie, 'docile' has only two syllables."

"Yeah? Well, check out this one-syllabus word." I drew in a huge gulp of air and roared a bark in his ear. ROOF! Heh heh. He jumped three feet straight up. I love doing that. "It means 'get to the point.' Are they dangerous or not? In other words, can I whip this guy?"

He gave me a hateful glare but didn't use any more big words on me. "Tree Sloths don't run, kick, bite, scratch, or claw. They're lazy and not very smart."

"Ha! Maybe he's a cat."

I thought that was pretty funny but Pete didn't even crack a smile. No surprise there. Cats have no sense of humor, none.

"Lighten up, Kitty, you take yourself way too seriously. By the way, I'm finished with my interrogation. Thanks for the information. One of these days, maybe I'll find you a little job with the Security Division..." I gave him a wink, "...

hauling trash. Ha ha."

I whirled around and marched away, leaving Kitty Precious to sulk and play with his tail. He looked irritated, even mad, but did I care? No. Pleasing cats isn't part of my job. In fact, there's an ancient piece of Cowdog Wisdom that says, "If the cats are happy, something's wrong."

If Pete was in a sulky mood, that meant that the rest of us were having a great day.

I was a proud dog when I marched away from the Interrogation Room, and why not? Hey, using my heartless interrogation techniques, I had broken down the scheming little wretch and dragged some very important information out of him. Here, let's review the Clue List. I guess we have time.

> **First Important Clue:** We had two independent witnesses claiming that our ranch had been invaded by an unauthorized creature, a Three-Toed Tree Slipper...unless you multiply toes times feet and then it becomes a Twelve-Toed Whatever. Use your own judgment here. I don't care what we call him.
>
> **Second Important Clue:** Regardless of how many toes they have, Tree Slobs eat trees, and we're talking about eating them right down to the ground. Sawdust. Total

destruction.

Third Important Clue: They tend to be lazy and dumb, therefore…

Fourth and Most Important Clue: I could whip him!

Heh heh. This would be an in-and-out job with no major bloodshed, and that was crucial information, because…well, a dog should always try to avoid a fair fight. Studies have shown that fair fights can cause facial swelling and aching

muscles, so we try to avoid them.

Pretty impressive, huh? You bet. I had won a huge moral victory over Sally May's rotten little cat and had gathered the kind of information that would give my career a tremendle boots....a tremendous boost, let us say. When I thrashed the Tree Sloth and saved ranch trees from destruction, my people would be thrilled. I would win gasps of delight, pats on the head, and maybe even a few steak dinners.

In other words, I had extracted all the information I needed to pursue the case, and was ready to move into Stage Two. But as I was marching away in triumph, I heard Pete's voice again, and it stopped me in my tracks. Hang on, you won't believe this part.

He said, this is a direct quote, he said, "Oh, one more thing, Hankie. It's all a fabrication."

I did a one-eighty and marched back to him. "What did you say?"

"It's all a fabrication, Hankie. That's a big word, but I'm sure you know what it means."

"Of course I do, but do you? What does it mean?"

"It means..." He fluttered his eyelids, probably because he knew it gets on my nerves. "It's a joke."

"What!"

"Just a nasty little trick, Hankie. I was bored."

BORED? For a moment, I was speechless. "You mean...you mean there was no mysterious creature eating trees?"

"It was a porcupine, Hankie, just a porcupine. There's no such thing as a Three-Toed Tree Sloth. Hee hee. Have a nice day."

He turned and went slithering back to the iris patch, snickering every step of the way. I was shattered. I felt as though someone had dropped a bomb down the stovepipe of my mind.

With great difficulty, I made my way up the hill to the machine shed. There, I flopped down in front of the sliding double doors and sifted through the wreckage. It appeared that the case I had spent so much time and effort piecing together had been blown to smithereens. Here, look at this.

Mysterious creature eating trees.
Beaver with a bad haircut.
Three-Toed Tree Sloth.
Porcupine.
Huh
?

You see how the clues form the shape of a funnel? That's the Funnel of Logic, a secret technique we use in Security Work. In fact, come to think about it, it's so secret, I shouldn't be

50

talking about it or showing our blueprints to the public. If this information reached the wrong eyes and ears, it could be very bad.

Tell you what, let's forget that we ever had this conversation, okay? It's just too secret. Sorry.

CHAPTER SIX

The Double-Dirty-Trick Trick

T ell you what, we'll go on with this, but please don't share it with anyone. I'm not kidding, it's VERY secret."

Okay, you've gotten a peek at the Funnel of Logic, which is so highly classified that very few people or dogs in the entire world are aware that it even exists. You will notice that the top end is wide, and that the entire structure "funnels down" to the narrow part at the bottom.

Very clever design. See, we load all our clues into the top end, stir it around, add a pinch of a rare spice whose name I can't reveal, and let it sit for thirty minutes. When time expires, we're supposed to get one drop of Pure Truth at the bottom-end of the funnel and it's supposed to give us the solution to a difficult case.

This time, what came out the bottom of the Funnel of Logic was a big fat question mark, and it appeared that my case had been destroyed. It lay in ruins all around me.

How could this have happened? I had worked SO HARD gathering clues and building the case, only to have it all swept away by my worst enemy in the whole world. He had lured me into a dirty trick!

I wasn't sure I could carry on with my work. I mean, when we invest heart and soil into a case of this magnetron, then watch it go dripping down the Drain of Life, it's hard to carry on.

Sometimes a dog just wants to give up, quit. Go back to bed. Retire from the Force. Go into exile.

I was in the midst of these gloomy thoughts when I heard footsteps approaching. Oh no, was it the rooster again? I glanced toward the sound and saw little Drover, bouncing along and wearing his usual silly grin.

"Oh, hi." He stopped and gave me a closer look. "Gosh, what's wrong with you?"

"Oh, nothing much. The world just collapsed on top of me."

He glanced around. "I'll be derned. I don't see anything."

"The wounds are inside, Drover. My irrigation of the cat turned out to be a complete disaster."

"Yeah, he hates water."

"Of course he hates water. All cats hate water." There was a moment of silence. "Why did you bring up water?"

"Well, you said you irrigated the cat, and I thought…"

"Drover, I *interrogated* the cat. In-ter-ro-ga-ted. It has nothing to do with water."

"Yeah, but…"

"Have you had your ears checked lately?"

"Well, let me think…"

"Open your mouth and say, 'Ahhh." He opened his mouth and I peered inside. "No wonder you can't hear anything. I can't even see your ears! What have you done with them?"

"Gwckd wcalske gkehbl."

"What? Speak up."

"Cslekci gugg rickle mumble bum."

"I can't understand a word you're saying. Close your mouth and try it again."

He closed his mouth. "I said, my ears are on the outside of my head."

I looked and, hmm, sure enough, there were

two ears. "Okay, I've found them."

"Oh good. I feel better now, how about you?"

I collapsed. "I don't feel better. How could I feel better? The cat destroyed my case."

"I'll be derned. Which one?"

"The Case of the Tree-Legged Tree Toad."

"Oh, you mean the porcupine?"

There was a long, throbbing moment of silence as I stared into the Great Emptiness of his eyes. "You knew?"

"Oh yeah, Pete told me it was just a dirty trick."

"And you kept that vital piece of information to yourself? Why didn't you tell me?"

"Oh, 'cause you never listen, I guess."

"Drover, how can I run the Security Division when nobody ever listens? The cat has made me look like an idiot and you went along with it!"

"Yeah, but..."

"You will be court-martialed for..." I cut my eyes to both sides. "Wait a second! The cat told you he was playing a dirty trick, right?"

"Which cat?"

"Pete, of course."

"Oh, him. Yeah, he was really proud of himself."

"I just figured this out. Ha! It wasn't just a dirty trick, son, it was the old Double Dirty Trick

Trick. Cats use it all the time."

"Yeah, but…"

I leaped to my feet. "Don't you get it? The little crook saw that I was only inches away from solving the case of the Tree Sloth and he couldn't stand it, so he fed us bogus information to throw us off the trail."

"Gosh, you mean…"

"Exactly. He was desperate and played the only card he had left. He invented the story about the porcupine, and you fell for it like a duck out of water."

"Yeah, but…"

"Even I got fooled. Oh, this is rich! He's the champion of dirty tricks and he almost pulled it off, but he forgot one thing, Drover. The mind of a dog is an awesome thing."

"I'm confused."

I whopped him on the back. "Shake it off, son. All you need to know is that we have the little sneak exactly where he wants us." His eyes crossed. "Please don't cross your eyes in the middle of my lecture. It's very distracting."

"Yeah, but…"

"Let's move out, we've got a job to do."

Wow, what a turn-around! Are you amazed that in mere minutes, I had exposed the cat's

Double Dirty Trick Trick? Hey, even I was surprised, I mean, the solution had come out of nowhere, and now it was time to activate all dogs and march off in search of the Tree Sloth.

I had never seen one with my own eyes, but our Department had compiled a file on its patterns and habits. We knew, for example, that Tree Sloths ate trees, so when our squadron reached the line of trees north of the ranch house (we called it the "shelter belt," remember?), when we reached the shelter belt, we slowed our pace and began looking for signs of tree-destruction, such as stumps and large piles of sawdust.

You're probably wondering why we weren't on the lookout for fallen trees. Tree Sloths eat 'em, that's why, so you never find the actual trees, only what's left—sawdust and maybe a few leaves.

Sure enough, we found no fallen trees, irreguffable proof that the Tree Sloth was chewing down our trees and eating them alive.

Actually, we didn't find any piles of sawdust either. That puzzled me at first, but then I figured it out. To conceal his presence on the ranch, the villain was not only devouring the trees but eating the piles of sawdust as well. This guy was a real pro.

As we crept through the half-darkness of the shelter belt, Drover came to a sudden stop and pointed to a tree up ahead of us. "Oh my gosh, look at that!"

I turned my Visual Scanners toward the tree and pulled it into focus. I saw...well, not much. "What are we looking at?"

"See those limbs? Bare."

"Holy smokes, quick, hit the ground! Turn out the lights and don't speak to strangers!" I hit the ground but Drover didn't move. "Hey, pal, bears eat dogs!"

He gave me a silly grin. "Yeah, but I didn't see a bear."

"Drover, I heard you say..."

"No, I said, those limbs are," he stuck his mouth next to my ear and yelled, "BARE!"

I gave him a shove backward. "Stop screeching in my ear! Do you think I'm deaf?"

"No, but you never listen. Look at those limbs."

"Don't give me orders!"

"Hank, just look at the limbs. They're bare. Something's been chewing the bark."

I narrowed my eyes and studied the tree. "Hmm. Something has chewed all the bark off those limbs and left them bare."

"That's what I said."

"That's NOT what you said. You turned in a confusing report about grizzly bears. How can I run the Security Division when I'm getting bad information?" I cut my eyes from side to side. "Drover, do you know what kind of animal eats the bark off of trees?"

"Yeah, porcupines."

"Not porcupines. Tree Sloths. We've got a live one. All we have to do is smoke him out and make the arrest. Okay, soldier, let's check for tracks."

We put our noses to the ground and began searching for tracks. See, when a wild animal passes through an area, he leaves tracks, footprints. This happens because animals walk on legs and their legs are attached to feet and their feet leave impressions in the dirt.

Legs, feet, tracks. See the pattern? It happens every time.

A lot of intruders think they can slip onto my ranch without being detected. What they don't know is that a highly-trained cowdog can do a Snifferation Test and find all sorts of tracks.

And, bingo, after a thirty-second Snifferation, I found one. "Here we go, I've got him on radar! Look at this."

Drover squinted down at the track. "I'll be derned. Four toes."

"What? That's impossible. A Three-Toed Tree Sloth can't leave a four-toed track." I looked closer and studied the track. Hmmm. Four toes.

"And you know what? It kind of looks like…a porcupine track."

You know what? It did, and that sent my mind into a swirl.

A lot of your ordinary mutts would have quit the case right there. In other words, they would have fallen for the obvious. Not me. Long experience in dealing with cats and crinimals had taught me NEVER TO FALL FOR THE OBVIOUS.

It was a brilliant ploy, I had to give him credit. It might have worked on some ordinary mutt, but not on me.

I glanced over both shoulders and dropped my voice to a whisper. "Drover, this guy is smarter than we thought."

"He is?"

"Yes. Obviously he has equipped himself with…"

Wait. I know you're aching to hear the rest of this, but we've got to change chapters. I'm sorry, but that's just the way it works around here. We have pages and we have chapters, and they're not the same.

So here's the deal: don't move, stay right there.

I'll take care of a few little housekeeping chores and we'll get back together on the other side. Believe me, it'll be worth the wait.

You absolutely won't believe this next part.

CHAPTER SEVEN

The Plot Plottens

I'm back, how about you? Good. I'm back, you're back, and we're ready to roll this case up into a nice little bundle.

Okay, Drover and I were in the shelter belt, north of the ranch house, and we had just discovered a mysterious track in the dust. It had been made by a creature with four toes, and Drover leaped to the conclusion that it was a porcupine track.

"I'm sorry, son, but you've been sand-bagged."

"I have?"

"Don't you get it? That track was left by a Three-Toed Tree Sloth—only he was equipped with a high-tech device that left exactly the kind of track we *weren't* looking for!"

"You mean…"

"Yes. Obviously he's equipped himself with prosthetic shoes."

Drover's eyes bugged out. "Prosthetic shoes?"

"Exactly. They were scientifically designed to leave a four-toed track. He's doing this to confuse us."

"Where would he buy shoes?"

"Drover, I deal in large concepts, not sniveling details. The large concept here is that our adversary wanted to throw us off the trail, so he left us some phony tracks. It was the smart play, very clever, but it didn't work."

"I'll be derned." He sniffed the track. "It even smells like a porcupine."

"See? Exactly my point. These guys will do anything to conceal their true identity." I began loosening up the muscles in my enormous shoulders. "Well, I've seen enough. How about you?"

"Oh, I wouldn't mind checking it out some more."

"Well, that's exactly the wrong answer. We've done all the checking we need to do. We've built a solid case and now it's time to send in the troops."

"Okay, good luck."

I paced a few steps away from the runt. "We're putting out a call for volunteers. We need a few good men to creep forward and scout those trees."

His eyes went blank. "Volunteers?"

"That's correct. And I've held a spot open for...YOU."

"Me! You said 'good men.' I'm just a dog."

"Drover, we're willing to waive some of the requirements."

"Yeah, and I'll wave goodbye!"

He tried to escape, but I knew his tricks and blocked his path. "Drover, this could be a great opportunity to advance your career."

"Yeah, but this leg's acting up again. I'm not sure I could stand the pain." He began limping around in circles. "See? Terrible pain!"

"Drover, pain is what drives us."

"Yeah, and it's driving me crazy! Oh, my leg!"

"Pain is the magic fuel that propels us to greater heights."

PLOP! He hit the ground like a rock. "Darn the luck, there it went!"

I glared down at him. "All right, you little slacker, if you won't volunteer, I'll volunteer for you. Get up. You have just been promoted to the Scout Patrol. Go do your duty. And never forget, son, this is for the ranch!"

And so it was that Drover volunteered to lead the Scout Patrol and go in search of the elusive Three-Tiered Toad Sloth. We knew it would be a dangerous mission and that some of our troops might not come back alive, but Drover stood tall and took the assignment.

Or, to come at it from another direction, he did his very best to weasel out of it, but I was able to coax him into taking the job. Heh heh. I used a motivational technique we call Brute Force. It worked.

He was shivering all over when I gave him his final instructions. "All right, men, sneak into that line of trees and check things out."

"It's awful dark in there."

"That's correct, and don't forget that it's always darkest before it gets any darker."

His teeth were clacking together. "Yeah, but what if I see a bear?"

"Drover, if you see a bear, you will go straight to your room and stand with your nose in the corner for three weeks. Do you know why? Because we have no bears on this ranch."

"Yeah, but..."

"Hush. Your orders for this mission are to find a Tongue-Tied Tree Sloth. Nothing else will do. If you're not back in five minutes, we'll extend the deadline and give you another thirty minutes. Now get with the program and do your stuff!"

He didn't go cheerfully but that was okay. We

prefer that our troops go into combat with a smile, but when they don't…well, we really don't care.

He crept into the dense grove of trees and soon disappeared into the shadows. I had to wait. This is always the hardest time for the commanding officer—the hours of waiting and worrying about the safety of the men, pacing back and forth, studying maps, going over every detail of the assignment and hoping that we didn't miss anything important.

It's tough, let me tell you, and sometimes it goes on for hours. Not this time. Two minutes after he left on patrol, he came scampering out of the trees.

I greeted him with bared fangs. "Get back in those trees and finish the mission! And I don't want to hear about your bad leg."

He was excited, hopping up and down and wig-wagging his stub tail. "I found him!"

"What? You mean…"

"Yeah, he's in the shelter belt, just like you said."

"You saw the Tree Sloth? Was he in a tree?"

"Well…not exactly. He was on the ground, chewing on a tree trunk."

"That's close enough. How about toes? Did you count his toes?"

"Well…"

"Excellent! He had three toes on each of his four feet, giving us the expected total of twelve toes. Am I right?"

"Well..."

"Great! It matches our profile. It's the Tree Sloth."

Drover rolled his eyes around. "Well...you know, he kind of looked like...a porcupine."

I couldn't hide my excitement. "Of course he did! Didn't I tell you? *He's disguised himself as a porcupine!* First he used the prosthetic shoes, now he's wearing the complete disguise. These guys are clever beyond our wildest dreams."

Wow, what a triumph! Drover's report of the scouting mission proved, without the slightest doubt, that we had located the villain. Even more important, it proved that the profile I had developed before the mission was correct in every detail, right down the line.

Bingo!

I was so excited, I could hardly contain myself, but Drover didn't seem to understand the murgitude of this triumph. He sat there, shaking his head and mumbling under his breath.

"What's wrong with you?"

"I think it's a porcupine."

I searched for patience. "Okay, I'll go over this

one last time, and please pay attention. If you had told me that the creature looked like a Tree Sloth, I would have known the whole mission was a failure. That would have meant that he was a beaver or a possum, wearing a sloth disguise."

"This is crazy. He looked just like a porcupine."

"Drover, open your eyes! That's proof that he *isn't*! You have to put yourself inside the crinimal mind, and see the world as he sees it."

"Yeah, but everything comes out backwards."

"Exactly my point. They use backwards logic to confuse us, but this time, we're one step behind them."

He blinked his eyes. "What do we do now?"

My mind was racing so fast, I had to pause a moment to slow it down. "We bust down the door, raid the joint, make the arrest, put him in cuffs, and escort him off the property."

"Yeah, but I didn't see a door."

I gave that some thought. "Good point. Okay, we won't bust it down."

"Yeah, 'cause if there's not a door, we can't bust it down."

"Exactly." I gave him a pat on the shoulder. "Son, you're starting to catch onto this business. It makes me proud to see you taking some insnickitive."

"Thanks. What's insnickitive?"

"It means that after all these years, you're finally starting to use your head for something besides a hat rack."

He grinned. "Yeah, I might as well use it. It's paid for."

I stared at him for a long moment. "You bought a hat?"

"No, my head's paid for. I was making a joke, but I guess it wasn't all that funny."

"I guess not." I glanced around in a full circle. "What were we talking about before you got us on the subject of hats?"

"Well, let me think here. Oh yeah, insnickitive."

"I never heard of it. What is it, a disease?"

"Yeah, I think it's kind of like rutabaga."

"Well, there is seldom a good excuse for rude behavior." The seconds ticked by and I began to fidget. "I think we were discussing something important. Do you remember what it was?"

He began scratching his left ear. "Well, let me think. Food?"

"Maybe that was it." I began pacing again. "Food is a very important subject for us dogs. Why? Because if it weren't for food, we'd have nothing to eat."

"I never thought that."

"Yes, well, it's true and..." I stopped in my tracks. "We weren't discussing food. We were in the middle of something very important, but I can't remember what it was."

I don't know how Drover does this, but it happens fairly often. At the very moment when I need to focus all my mental powers like a laser bean, he starts babbling nonsense. Sometimes, out of pity for the runt, I try to show some interest in his little nothings and the next thing I know... poof! I lose the track of my train.

I lose my train tracks.

I lose my train of thought, let us say.

It's more than annoying. It's frustrating and embarrassing. I've thought of firing him, you know. I've kept him on the payroll for years and often find myself lying awake and thinking, "Why do I do this to myself?" Why don't I just call him into my office and give him the straight truth?

Something like, "Drover, we've been reviewing the files on all our employees. We've noticed that your file is *empty*. You've been with the Security Division for how many years? And the records show that you've done ABSOLUTELY NOTHING. I'm sorry, we have to let you go. Clear out your desk. Goodbye."

That would be the sensible course of action,

but I've never been able to pull it off. Why? He would cry. I know he would cry. That would be So Drover: sniffle, whimper, sob, bawl, screech, and drip tears all over my desk.

And then I would be tortured by feelings of guilt. What would his mother say when she learned that her son had turned out to be the bum she'd always thought he was? It would break her heart, and then she would cry too.

My dreams would be filled with the howls and moans of Drover and all his kinfolks. I would never get any sleep, my productivity would take a nosedive, the entire Security Division would go into a steep decline...and who needs that?

I get all the worries, cares, and responsibilities and he gets a free ride.

Even so, one of these days I will have to fire him, otherwise I'll be stuck with him forever. In many ways, this is a lousy job, but the impointant point is that I have no idea what we were talking about, and it makes me so mad, I could spit.

Let's change chapters again. Sometimes that helps to clear the fog from the bog.

CHAPTER EIGHT

Bad News For The Runt

~~~~~~

Good news, it worked. That little break allowed me to grab some fresh air and restore my bodily fluids, and I remember exactly what we were talking about: the Tree Sloth. Now we're cooking. Let's get organized and rush back to the case.

Okay, there we were in a dark grove of trees north of ranch headquarters, in the midst of one of the most important investigations of my whole career. We were about to launch Operation Yellow Mayonnaise.

If you recall, I had sent one of our agents out on a scouting mission and our Intelligence Section had done a complete analysis of his paralysis. It revealed a clear picture. We had a live Tree Sloth running loose. We had him on radar, we had him on sonar, and our agent had caked the icing with a first-hand, boots-on-the-ground, eye-witness observation.

I turned to my assistant and looked him straight in the eyes. "All right, men, the time has come. We're going in, but Drover, I've got some bad news."

"Oh darn. I hate bad news."

"I'm sorry."

"You're welcome."

"Thanks."

"You're welcome."

"Will you please hush? How can I give you the bad news if you're babbling?"

He hung his head. "Sorry. Go ahead, I guess I'm ready."

While he hung his head and quivered, I paced a few feet away and gazed off into the distance. "Drover, we've been reviewing all our personnel files."

"Uh oh."

"And, well, we came to yours."

"How was it?"

"It was depressing. I hate to put it that way, but it's the truth. All these years you've been with the Security Division and our files show that you've done…nothing!"

He hung his head and nodded. "I was hoping you wouldn't notice."

"I've tried not to notice. I've tried to ignore all the half-stepping and gold-bricking, but there comes a time when the worm of truth emerges from the apple of life."

"Yeah, I had worms once. They're pretty bad."

"Don't try to distract me. I don't care that you had worms. We're talking about your record of service here at the Security Division, and the terrible truth is…you don't have a record of service!"

He blinked his eyes and a tear slid down his cheek. "So…I guess I'm fired?"

I marched over to him and gave him a steely gaze. "You're not fired, but I'm taking you off this case."

He stared at me. "Really?"

"You heard me. I will serve as the arresting officer."

"You mean…"

"Yes. Your scouting report helped build our case against the Tree Sloth, but I'm taking it from here. Do you know why?"

"Well, let me think…"

"I'm taking over the case because you don't deserve the glory of making the arrest. No one in the history of the Security Division has ever compiled such a dismal record!"

"You mean...I can't get into a fight with the Tree Sloth?"

"That's correct. You're off the case...and why are you grinning?"

"Who, me? I wasn't grinning."

"You *were* grinning, I saw it myself."

"Oh, that? I was grinning to keep from crying."

"Oh. Well, I guess that makes sense. I know this must come as a shock."

"Yeah, it really hurts."

"If it'll make you feel better, go ahead and cry. Let it all hang out."

"Okay." He covered his face with his paws and broke into sobs. "Hee hee hee!"

Those of us in Security Work see tragedy all the time and everyone thinks we don't have feelings. Well, we do, but we have to toughen ourselves to protect our emotional so-forths. If we let every little barb of sadness penetrate our Inner Bean, we wouldn't be able to carry on with our work.

I didn't cry but my mist musted over...my eyes misted over, let us say, and I felt the sadness almost as deeply as Drover did. At last I went to him and laid a paw upon his shoulder. "It's time to begin the mission. I must go. You stay behind and try to be brave."

Before my emotions could over-swamp me, I rushed away. As I marched off to battle, I heard his sobs of pain.

"Hee hee hee!"

The poor little guy! He deserved to be booted off the case, but still...I guess some dogs enjoy being mean and cruel, making others squirm and cry, but I've never developed a taste for it myself.

Sometimes I have to be heartless, but I don't enjoy it. Drover would never know that this was hurting me almost as much as it was hurting him. I had to put it out of my mind and concentrate on my mission.

As I moved deeper into the grove of trees, the sunlight faded and I found myself creeping through a forest of dark shadows. I switched all circuits into Stealthy Crouch Mode, raised both Forward Antennas, activated Smelloradar, and followed a westerly course that would take me from Point A to Point B.

If you're not familiar with the complicated business of navigation, you're probably wondering how I knew there would be a Point B out there in the darkness of those trees. I mean, we're talking about some pretty spooky darkness and shadows, right?

We don't have time to go into all the technical details, so let me just say that one of the rules we learn in Navigation School is: if you have a Point A, you can usually find a Point B.

Do you know why? It's pretty simple, actually, if you stop and think about it. Point A is where you start the mission, and Point B is where you end up. Every mission has a beginning and an end. Therefore, following the path of simple logic...

Maybe this is obvious.

That brings us to the scary part. Are you ready? I hope so.

I stalked and stealthed my way through the jungle of trees. Off in the distance, I heard the blood-chilling scream of a tiger, then the thunderous roar of a bull moose. Did the elusive Tree Sloth make any kind of scream or bellow? We just didn't know. All we had to work with was our Tree Sloth Profile: a lumbering, awkward, dull-witted creature that eats trees.

Suddenly... hang on... suddenly, something moved in front of me, an animal...a furry animal with long ears. I sent this information to Data Control. Seconds later, a report flashed across the screen of my mind:

"COTTONTAIL RABBIT"

Whew! False alarm.

I heaved a sigh of relief and continued my creeping march through the trees and shadows and shadowy trees. Time moved slowly. Every muscle in my highly-conditioned body ached with tension. On and on. I had just begun to think that the mission might end in failure when...

I saw him! There he was, a lumbering, dull-witted creature gnawing on a tree trunk. He had four legs, a fat tail, and a pair of dull yellow eyes. And just as I had expected, he was wearing a porcupine disguise!

Just to make sure he was the Tree Sloth, I entered all the data into our onboard computer. Suddenly the screen began flashing:

THREE-TOED TREE SLOTH!
Confirmed!
Prepare To Engage!

Okay, this was it, the moment every ranch dog lives for and waits for, the moment when he can funnel all the tunnels of his savage energy into one blazing point of light, and go charging into combat against...well, a slow, lumbering, dull-witted creature who probably isn't a great fighter.

Let's be honest here. We dogs have to be realistic. Combat is fun, but the weaker the foe, the funner the fun. I mean, the objective of every combat mission is to WIN. Would you rather fight a grizzly bear and get the stuffings whipped out of you, or fight a lazy, bumbling Tree Sloth and come out with a glorious victory for the ranch?

It's not rocket surgery.

Yes, this would be a great little fight. The elite troops of the Security Division would win an overwhelming victory and bring honor and glory to the ranch—all without a great loss of blood, hair, or skin.

Too bad little Drover would have to miss all the fun. I could still hear the sound of his sobbing: "Hee hee hee!"

CHAPTER NINE

The Law of Gravy

Was I ready? Was I up to the task? You bet I was!

I announced my presence with a loud bark, which resembled the blast of a bugle. The Tree Sloth lifted his head and glanced around, and you won't believe this part. He didn't show any signs of fear. In fact, he gave me a lazy grin and said, "Oh, hi. You must be the guard dog."

"That's correct. Hank the Cowdog, Head of Ranch Security."

He lifted a paw in greeting. "Hi there. I'm Buzzy. I think we've met before."

"Not likely. I can't remember names but I always forget a face. Take my word for it, we haven't met."

He chuckled. "Yeah, we've met. It was down by the creek, dark night. You came roaring up, barking your fool head off, and I told you to back off. You didn't, of course. Typical dog."

"I'll say it one more time. We haven't met."

"Whatever you think." He pointed to the tree trunk. "I was just having some breakfast. You want a bite?"

"I don't eat trees, Buddy, so let's skip the small talk and go straight to the bottom line." I leaned toward him and dropped my voice to a menacing growl. "We've had you under surveillance for weeks, pal, and we know who you are."

"Well, that's good. I was Buzzy the first time we met, and I still am."

"Well, that's your story. You want to hear the truth?"

He stared at me with his dull-witted eyes. "Now you've got me curious. Sure."

"You're not a porcupine."

"I'm not?"

"No. It's an ingenious disguise, but not good enough."

He scowled. "Huh. If I ain't a porcupine, you need to tell my momma."

"Are you trying to be funny?"

"No, she's a porcupine and she thinks I'm one

too."

"That's clever, Buddy, but it won't work."

"My name's Buzzy. Buzz-zee."

"I know your name, pal, it's in our database."

"Then quit calling me Buddy." He moved back to the tree and began chewing the bark. "You know, these chinaberry trees have kind of a bitter taste."

"Stop eating my tree. Now."

He gave me a lazy glance. "I thought you was joking. Maybe not."

"No jokes and no more breakfast. Back away from the tree and clear out. If you don't, I'll have to make an arrest."

"An arrest? Me?"

"That's correct, and I must warn you, it could get messy."

He frowned and began rubbing the top of his head with a paw. "Now, let me get this straight. You think I ain't a porcupine, is that what you said?"

"Correct. I *know* you're not."

"Well, if I ain't a porcupine, how come I'm wearing all these quills?"

I laughed. "Like I said, it's a great disguise and it would fool an ordinary dog. The quills almost look real."

"There's a reason for that." He gave me a

wink. "They almost look real 'cause they ARE, and the last time we had this conversation, you got a college education."

I moved closer and showed him some fangs. "Last chance. Do yourself a favor and clear out."

He heaved a sigh and looked off in the distance. "Now doggie, I've got no quarrel with you. I'm going to finish my breakfast. You just run along and chase a chicken and we'll all have ourselves a good day."

"That's your last word?"

"Yup."

"Very well. Hands up, you're under arrest!" I couldn't believe it. He ignored me! "A hard-head, huh? Okay, you asked for this!"

I didn't wanted to hurt the dummy, but he'd left me no choice. I loosened up the muscles in my enormous shoulders, went into the Deep Crouch Position, hit the Launch button, and exploded into the air.

He had been warned. My conscience was...

HUH?

You know, high altitude sometimes gives you an entirely different perspective on things. On the ground, Buzzy had looked exactly like a Three-Tiered Tree Sloth wearing a porcupine suit. From the air, he began to resemble...

Yipes, those quills looked real, sharp, and really sharp, and there were thousands of them! Suddenly, very suddenly, I found myself experiencing a Flash of Insight.

Hadn't I met this guy before?

Yes, maybe more than once.

And when we'd met before, he wasn't a Tree Sloth or any other kind of sloth.

He'd been a...gulp.

Suddenly and all at once, all the facts and memories seemed to be pointing like a flaming arrow toward a conclusion that I really didn't want to hear.

I felt the hair rising on the back of my neck. I snatched up the microphone of my mind and screamed, "Mayday, mayday! Drover, at this moment I am airborne and heading straight for a porcupine! Send in the reserves! This is not a drill!"

The radio crackled and I heard a distant voice: "Yeah, that's what I thought."

"Never mind what you thought, we need heavy artillery and fresh troops at once! Do you copy?"

The radio went dead and so did my hopes.

Oh brother.

You know, once a guy has made a great leap

into the air and has begun his downly deadward spiral...his deadly downward spiral, that is, there isn't a whole lot he can do in the way of course correction. The Law of Gravy has no favorites and it doesn't care whether we believe in it or not.

The Law of *Gravity*, it should be. There is no Law of Gravy, except that it's delicious. In fact, some of my most cherished memories came from evening Scrap Events that involved roast beef trimmings and beef gravy. Wonderful stuff.

Where were we? Oh yes, the Law of Gravy. The mathematical so-forth behind this law was worked out many years ago by the famous scientist Sir Figgy Newton. After an apple fell upon his head, he wondered, "If they can make apple sauce out of apples, why not apple gravy?" And that question shook the scientific...

Wait, forget the apples. I was in the midst of a deadly downward spiral, remember? You need to work on your concentration.

Okay, when a dog begins that fateful plunge, he can try to swim like a fish or fly like a bird, and it won't make the list beet of difference. What he discovers is that you can't swim out of water and that dogs don't fly.

This is very embarrassing. In fact, it's so embarrassing that I'm not going to finish the story. The little children must never know...

That's all I can say. I'm signing off. Goodbye.

[Long Period of Silence]

You're still here. What's the deal? I thought we decided that the story had gotten too scary for the little children, remember? Yes, we talked it over and decided that the kids weren't quite old enough to hear...well, the truth, you might say.

But you're still here and so am I. Do we dare go on with the story? It's liable to be pretty shocking.

CHAPTER TEN

Quills!

Are you still with me? Tell you what, let's send the younger kids to bed and we'll see how it goes with the older ones. They might do okay. Kids are tougher than you think.

So let's go ahead and send the little guys off to bed, and remind them to brush their teeth. That's very important. Nobody needs dirty teeth.

Oh, and tell 'em to use dental floss.

Have we cleared the room? Good. Gather around and let's get this over with. It's going to be very painful. Nobody likes to admit...

Okay, remember all those reports that had come into the Security Division? We'd been told that some kind of exotic animal was running wild on my ranch, a Toad-Footed Tree Sloth. Our information indicated that he was eating ranch trees and might be a secret agent for the Charlie Monsters. We feared that he might even be involved in some kind of plot to take over the ranch.

Oh, and don't forget that our agents reported that this villain often disguised himself as a porcupine. No kidding, that's what we were hearing, that he was dressed up in a porcupine suit and wearing special shoes that left phony porcupine tracks.

There was only one problem with those reports. They were pure GARBAGE, nothing but a pack of lies that were designed to lure me into a very embarrassing encounter with...grab hold of something solid, here it comes...a very embarrassing encounter with a PORCUPINE.

Yes, he was a real in-the-flesh, no-joke porcupine, and we might as well move along with the rest of the story. It's bad news. I jumped right in the middle of a porcupine named Buddy. He was kind of a pleasant fellow. We had a little chat and argued about his name.

He insisted that he was a porcupine. I should have listened, because he knew what he was talking about. I discovered that he had no sense of humor. Zero. And I made another important discovery: all porcupines are equal when you

jump on them. They don't growl, bark, hiss, scratch, or bite. They don't laugh or brag or mouth off. They just stand there and let the dog...

We really don't need to go into every ugly detail of this encounter. Bottom line: it was a short fight and when it was over, Buddy waddled off into the trees and I was left wearing a hundred and thirty-seven porcupine quills.

You're probably wondering, "How does a dog respond to this kind of crisis?" Great question. I mean, porcupine quills can be a real problem. When a dog is wearing them, he can't do a lot of the things he normally would like to do, such as eat, drink, and be merry, bark, bite, and chew a bone.

Everything becomes painful. See, every time you try to do something that involves your mouth or nose, you bump against those quills, which drives them deeper into your cheeks, gums, lips, and nose. And those quills HURT.

Your ordinary dogs will see this as a hopeless situation. I mean, when your mouth and nose get taken out of the game, what's left? Not much. Hencely, your ordinary mutts will close up the store, so to speak, and go looking for one of the cowboys...and beg for help.

"Help" in this situation means sitting perfectly still while a cowboy pulls out the quills with a pair of pliers.

Not me, fellers. In the first place, I never beg, not for help or anything else. The Head of Ranch Security *does not beg*, period. In the second place, getting de-quilled with a pair of pliers hurts like crazy. The cowboys on this outfit have all the charm and bedside manner of a butcher, and who needs that?

In the third place—and this might be the most impointant—when a dog submits to the de-quilling process, he is forced to listen while the cowboys moan and bellyache, such as: "Hank, for crying in the bucket, how many times do you have to jump on a porcupine before you figure it out!"

That's the kind of trash we have to listen to around here. You make one little mistake and they never let you forget it.

Okay, let's be honest. Maybe this wasn't my first experience with a porcupine. Maybe it had happened once before...several times, but let me hasten to point out that this was the first time I had ever jumped on a porcupine that was masquerading as a Tree Sloth.

This was a completely different situation, but there was no way I could explain it to Slim and Loper. They just wouldn't understand.

Dogs have had this problem with their masters since the beginning of time. Humans have no idea how complicated life can be for a dog, and their answer to everything seems to be...well, that dogs are just dumb.

I knew that's what they would say and I didn't need to hear it. And that was the main reason I made my decision NOT to seek medical attention for my Quill Problem. No, by George, I would take care of it myself.

I went straight to my office under the gas tanks, fluffed up my gunny sack bed, did the usual Three Turns Maneuver around the bed, and dropped into its warm embrace. My plan was to quarantine myself from the rest of the world, ignore the pain, and wait for...well, wait for the quills to fall out, go away, and leave me alone.

In other words, I would endure my suffering alone—one brave cowdog standing tall against the pain and humiliation of a Porcupine Assault. The first five minutes went pretty well, but then guess who showed up.

Drover. Just the guy I didn't want to see. I was badly messed up, but I didn't want any help or sympathy from him. I wanted only to be alone.

He plopped down on his gunny sack bed and for a long time he didn't say anything. Then he gave me a silly grin. "How's it going?"

I beamed him a flaming glare. "How do you think it's going, you little traitor!"

"Gosh, what did I do?"

"You allowed your commanding officer to go out on a suicide mission, that's what you did!"

"Yeah, but..."

"That creature wasn't a Tree Sloth. It was a deadly porcupine!"

"Yeah, I tried to warn you."

"Why didn't you warn me?"

"Well, I did, and so did Pete, but you never listen."

"How can I run this ranch when my own Security Division is riddled with spies and traitors!"

There was a long moment of silence. Then he said, "You've got a bunch of quills in your nose. Reckon you ought to get some help?"

"I will NOT go begging for help."

He was quiet for a moment. "You know, quills have little barbs, so they don't come out on their own."

"I don't care. I have my pride, Drover, and you know what else? I can tolerate pain, which is something you know nothing about."

"Yeah, I hate pain. It always seems so painful."

"Exactly my point. Pain is painful and that is the purpose of pain. It reminds us that there's more to this life than comfort and luxury."

He grinned. "Yeah, but I kind of like comfort and luxury."

"We're all drawn to the easy life, Drover, but we shouldn't be. Luxury will corrupt a dog, turn him into a poodle. Is that what you want, to be a poodle?"

"Well, I never thought about it. How's the nose?"

"The nose is great. You go right ahead and turn yourself into a pampered little yip-yip, if that's what you want. As for me..."

Ba-BOOM. Ba-BOOM. Ba-BOOM.

Hmmm, that was odd. I had just noticed a strange sensation in the soft leathery portion of my nose, almost as though...well, as though someone were inside, beating on a bass drum.

"Drover, do you hear a drum?"

He cocked one ear and listened. "Nope, can't hear a thing."

"This is strange. There for a second...wait, there it is again! I hear a bass drum and it seems to be centered...well, on the end of my nose. And here's another clue. With every boom of the drum, I can feel...well, in some ways it resembles...pain."

"I'll be derned, I don't feel anything." For a moment, he seemed lost in thought, then his eyes popped wide open. "Wait a second, I just figured it out. Your nose is starting to swell up from the quills."

"Rubbish. If my nose had begun to swell, I would be the first to notice."

"Yeah, but you said it was starting to hurt."

"I did not say that. I said..." Ba-BOOM! Ba-BOOM! "Drover, one last question. Do you have any idea where I might find Slim and Loper?"

"Well, let me think here." He squinted one eye and rolled the other one around. "Oh yeah, I saw 'em up at the machine shed. They just came back from the field."

I leaped to my feet. "Good. I have some business to attend to and I'm going to leave you in charge of the office."

"Who, me? Gosh, you'd better tell me what to do."

"I don't care what you do. Sleep, scratch a flea, I don't care." I began backing away. "Hold my calls. I'll be back in an hour. Two hours. Before dark."

And with that, I went in search of...remember our discussion about porcupine quills and pain? Someone had made the statement that quills don't hurt, or if they do, a dog should be able to stand the pain. I don't remember who said that, but I can tell you that it was total nonsense.

MY NOSE WAS KILLING ME!

Take the word of a dog who knows about quills. Not only do they sting like fire, but they can cause the noselary region to swell up and throb like a bass drum. Furthermore, quills have vicious little barbs that cause them to penetrate deeper and deeper into the innocent flesh of a dog's nose. If left unattended, they will do incredible damage.

Hencely, it should come as no surprise that I came to a sensible, mature decision about my Quill Situation. Even though I didn't wish to burden Slim and Loper with my problems, I went streaking up to the machine shed to find them.

Sure enough, they were working inside. Hammers clanged and the electric welder buzzed. Wait, hold everything! Was this some kind of hidden clue? The welder BUZZED and I had been attacked by a porcupine named BUZZY. Was it a mere accident that both words contained a rare Double Z?

Maybe it meant nothing. Just skip it.

Anyway, bright flashes of light from the welder twinkled through a cloud of smoke, and now and then I caught glimpses of two adult male cowboys working in the fog.

Apparently they had torn up some farming equipment in the field. They do that quite often, tear up the machinery, and then they try to fix it with the welder.

I walked up to the big sliding doors, which

were open. I stopped, stood there, and switched on a little program we call Loyal Dog Waiting Patiently, which we often use in times of need. I knew that in mere moments, they would look up from their work and notice that their Head of Ranch Security had been wounded in battle.

Ba-BOOM. Ba-BOOM.

Minutes passed and nobody came. Loyal Dog Waiting Patiently wasn't working. Those guys took hints like a buffalo, so I switched off LDWP and went to another program we call Pain, Woe, and Suffering. This required that we give them Mournful Looks and Slow Wags on the tail section...and moans.

Yes sir, loud moans, tragic moans, the kind of moans that will stop the world and cause rocks to burst into tears. "Aaaaa-OOOOOO! Aaaa-OOOOO!"

Those were some awesome moans and sure enough, the clanging and banging stopped. A moment later, Slim Chance stepped outside and raised the front of his welding hood. He looked around and scowled, but he didn't see me.

Hey! Right here, you tuna! It's me. I've been wounded in the line of duty and my nose is about to explode!

Aaaaa-OOOOOO!

At last...at long, long last, his gaze lit upon me. "Was that you?"

Yes, of course it was me! And would you please hurry up?

He grinned. "Oh. I thought we had a pig hung under a gate." He turned and went back inside. He didn't even see the quills! Hey!

This was an outrage. What did a dog have to do to get help around here?

I took a huge gulp of air and was about to cut loose with a window-shattering moan when... there he was again. Slim. He narrowed his eyes and took a closer look at me.

His eyes rolled upward. "Good honk, quills! Again?" He turned toward the inside of the barn and yelled, "Hey, Loper, come here and look at your dog. He's learned a trick."

A moment later, Loper appeared in the door, wiping his hands on a red grease rag. "What trick?"

Slim pointed a bony finger at me. "He talked a porcupine into loaning him some quills."

Loper gave me a blunt, ugly stare. His eyes rolled upward and he gave his head a slow shake. "I don't believe it. I do not believe this!"

Oh brother. See what I told you? Show up at the Emergency Room door and all they can do is gripe and moan, make jokes, and...phooey. I didn't have to take this kind of treatment.

I lifted my head to a proud angle, whirled around, and marched away from the scoffers and mockers. By George, I would cure my own quills, because I couldn't stand the thought of having to listen to them moan and bellyache about having to do a little bit of unpleasant work.

I mean, a dog has his pride. We get tired of their smart remarks and stale jokes, so I did what any normal, healthy American dog would have done. I lifted my head to a dignified angle and walked away. Hey, if they didn't want my quill business, I would just...

Ba-BOOM! Ba-BOOM!

I would just swallow my pride and throw myself upon their mercy. What else can a poor dog do? We can't pull our own quills, so we have to...

It wasn't fun. It was embarrassing but it had to be done. I went back to them and...GROVELED. Yes, I groveled—lowered my head and tail, went to Big Droop on the ears and gave them Eyes of Shame and Remorse.

I hated it.

CHAPTER ELEVEN

Emergery Surgency

Would it work? It was hard to say. Their eyes had turned cold, so I gave them a Pitiful Porcupined Smile. And you know what? I think that clinched the deal.

Loper turned to Slim. "Get the pliers."

"You get the pliers. He's *your* dog."

"He's your dog. Get the pliers."

"Loper, I pulled quills last time."

"Yes, but you're forgetting a very important detail." An evil smile slithered across Loper's mouth, and he whispered, "I'm the boss and you're not."

Slim shifted the toothpick over to the other side of his mouth. "Loper, you make Simon LaGreasy look like Mother Turista."

Loper barked a laugh. "It's Simon LaGree and Mother Theresa."

"I don't care. The point is that somebody took out your heart and replaced it with a sack of rocks."

"Get the pliers and hurry up."

Slim stalked back into the machine shed and emerged with a pair of needle-nose pliers. And would you like to guess what he said? Do you suppose he said, "Hank, our dear and loyal friend, we have to rush you into surgery to save your nose"?

That's NOT what he said. He said, and this is a direct quote, he curled his lip at me and growled, "Come here, Bozo, let's get this over with."

So much for bedside manner. And who was Bozo? I've never been sure what that name means, but it seems to come up when the cowboys are in a bad mood.

And so the surgery began. It wasn't pretty or delicate. Dr. Dracula sat down on the cement floor and threw a leg lock around my middle. He moved the pliers toward my face and muttered, "Hang on, pooch, this might hurt."

Yes, I knew it would hurt, but I was ready. I steeled myself for the ordeal. When you get to be Head of Ranch Security, you have to deal with...

OW!!!

A jolt of fire burned a path through my entire body, starting at the soft leathery portion of my nose and going all the way out to the last three hairs on the tip of my tail. And suddenly there was an explosion of...well, ME, you might say.

I fought and struggled against the ropes and chains and boa constrictors that held me down. I churned and dug and clawed, struggled and strained, and then...well, it was over. Slim held up the last hateful quill and said, "That's all for today, pooch. We sure appreciate the business."

He thinks he's so funny, but he's not.

I picked myself and my wounded dignity off the floor and was about to march away, when I noticed that Slim was still sitting there, and staring at a big wet spot on his shirt and jeans.

His eyes came at me like bullets. "Meathead, look what you did!"

Me? Surely not. But on the other hand, pain affects us all in different ways and sometimes in the middle of surgery...

When I walked out of the hospital, I made a vow that, in the future, I would take my quill business somewhere else—not that I would ever get into another scuffle with a porcupine, but... well, a guy never knows.

Anyway, I left the operating room and walked out of the hospital, a new dog. Slim had gotten all wet and I didn't care. Hey, I was cured and felt like a million bucks!

Pretty amazing, huh? You bet.

So, yes, I was feeling grand as I headed back to

my office under the gas tanks. I was even looking forward to seeing Drover again, the little weenie, and getting started with his court-martial.

But wait...something was running toward me. A bird with feathers.

Oh no, it was the rooster again!

CHAPTER TWELVE

Paybacks

W here were we? Oh yes. The Case of the Free-Toed Tree Sloth turned out to be one of the toughest assignments of my whole career. After being mugged by a heartless porcupine, I had endured seven hours of surgery, performed by two of the most incompetent cowboy-doctors in the entire state of Texas.

And as I was leaving the operating room, I saw someone jogging toward me, someone I didn't want to see: J.T. Cluck, the Head Rooster.

I changed directions and hurried around to the east side of the machine shed. There, I ducked into some tall weeds and lay flat on the ground. Maybe he would think I just vanished, poof. That happens sometimes, right?

Here he came. I could hear his feet clicking on the gravel. "Hey, where'd you go? I've got some important news and you need to hear it." I flattened myself even more and went into the Invisible Dog program. The weeds crackled, then... "Oh, there you are. When did you start taking naps in the weeds?"

I had been exposed. I rose to my feet and showed him two rows of teeth. "I wasn't taking a nap. If you must know, I was trying to avoid YOU."

He cocked his head to the side and studied me with his reddish rooster eyes. "Well, that's kind of unfriendly. Why would you do that?"

I stepped out of the weeds and shook the leaves off my coat. "Because, J.T., there are times when I just can't tolerate any more news about your heartburn."

"Heartburn? Oh no, I got over that. The good thing about squash bugs is they don't last long. I've got a good gizzard, and when me and my gizzard go to work, we grind 'em up pretty quick. The secret is the gravel. You've got to keep plenty of gravel in your craw."

"Good. Well, it was nice seeing you." I walked away.

He followed. "Hey, I ain't finished. We've got things to talk about."

I stopped. "Two minutes. Get to the point, and I don't want to hear one word about your heartburn."

"Boy, you're awful crabby."

"Hurry up."

He looked from side to side and leaned toward me. "Pooch, me and Elsa had a long talk. You remember that strange creature she seen? The one that looked like a beaver with a bad haircut? Well, she figured it out."

"It wasn't a beaver with a bad haircut."

"That's right."

"It was a porcupine."

His beak dropped open. "How'd you know that?"

"Because, after you gave me your garbage report, I tracked him down and jumped into the middle of him."

"Well, that was dumb. I could have told you, they have sharp quills. A dog can get a snoot full of quills messing around with a porcupine."

"Yes, I noticed. Thanks to you and Elsa, I collected about a hundred of them."

J.T. shook his head. "Huh. I'll be jiggered. You know, her eyes ain't what they used to be. Sometimes she sees things. Why, just the other evening, she come a-running into the chicken house, clucking and a-flapping her wings. She said, 'Oh, J.T., oh my! There's a giant bullfrog right outside our front door!'"

I hated to show any interest in this mess, but I was curious. "So what was it?"

"Well, she got it half-right. It was a bull, not a frog, and he was plenty big. I went outside and told him to shoo."

"And?"

"Well, bulls don't shoo, and this one turned out to be..." All at once, his eyes popped wide open and he hiked up his left leg and started scratching under his wing. "It's those darned bugs again! They're eating me alive!"

"I'm out of here, J.T., and with any luck, we'll never speak again. Thanks again for the quills, and I hope you enjoy your bugs." I whirled around and marched away.

What a dunce. How do I get trapped into listening to stories about his empty little chicken-life? I know the answer. I'M TOO NICE. A dog in my position shouldn't waste a minute of his valuable time...oh well, I had survived the porcupine ordeal and was ready to fall into the embrace of my gunny sack bed.

I was trotting toward the gas tanks when my ears began picking up the sounds of...was that laughter? I stopped, lifted Earatory Scanners, and turned the antennas until they zeroed in on the sounds that appeared to be coming from the Laughter Bandwidth.

Even more surprising, they were coming from...my office in the Security Division's Vast Office Complex!

I switched on Infrared Detection and did a Visual Sweep.

HUH?

Holy smokes, it appeared that Drover was having a party in my office, and a stranger was sitting on my gunny sack bed!

Would you care to guess who or whom was occupying my place of honor? Don't guess, I'll tell you: my worst friend in the whole world, Pete the Barncat!

My blood pressure began to rise, and it rose even more when I began picking up their conversation on Earatory Scanners. Here's the transcript, word for word.

Pete: "So he actually believed it was a Three-Toed Tree Sloth?"

Drover: "Oh yeah, hee hee. He thought it was a sloth wearing a porcupine suit."

"A porcupine suit! Hee hee! Incredible! Who else would think of that? So he jumped on the porcupine?"

"Yeah, I tried to warn him, but you know Hank."

"Yes, even I tried to warn him. Amazing! So he got some quills in his nose, did he?"

"Oh yeah, about a thousand of 'em. He had to go up to the machine shed and..."

When Drover looked around and saw me looming outside the office, his traitorous little grin dropped like a dead pigeon out of the sky. His eyes grew as wide as grapefruits and he gasped. "Oh my gosh!"

Pete saw me too. "My, my, I think the cops are here."

I stepped forward. "That's right, Kitty. Turn out the lights, the party's over."

The little sneak threw a glance over his shoulder, checking out the escape routes. "Now, Hankie, let's don't be bitter. It was just a little joke."

"Was it?"

"Yes, but..." He snickered. "Actually, Hankie, I never dreamed you'd fall for it. I mean, a Three-Toed Tree Sloth? Hee hee. You have to admit it was pretty crazy."

I laughed and continued advancing toward the cat. He didn't know it, but I was entering Launch Data into the computer.

"Ha ha. It was a good prank, Pete. I have to give you credit. No one does dirty tricks better than a cat."

He began easing backwards. "Why, thank
you, Hankie. I work at it every day, you know."

"Yes, I know. You're a professional sneak and

sometimes you win a little victory, but in the long run, Pete, you're a loser."

"Oh really. I wonder what you mean by that."

My finger was twitching on the Launch Button. "Here's an idea. How would you like to spend the rest of the day in a tree?"

"You know, I'd rather not."

"Too bad. Up the tree, you little pest!"

I launched the weapon and we raced to the nearest chinaberry tree. He got there first and scrambled up to the top-most branch, and that's where I parked him for the rest of the day.

"There, let this be a lesson to you! Cheaters never win."

With that out of the way, I stormed back to the office to take care of the other traitor. Drover. When I got there, he was hopping up and down. "Way to go, Hankie, great job! Boy, you fixed him!"

"Thanks, and now I'm fixing to fix *you*. We'll skip the court-martial and go right to the bottom line. You will stand with your nose in the corner for three years."

"Three years! Yeah, but..."

"Go!"

And that's about the end of the story. I had solved the case, treed the cat, and cleaned all the spies and traitors out of the Security Division.

Pete spent a miserable day, yowling in a tree, and Drover spent the rest of his life, rotting in a dark prison cell.

Okay, he didn't exactly spend the rest of his life in prison. He whined and cried and said he was sorry for allowing a cat to sit on my bed, so after he'd served thirty minutes of his sentence, I...well, had a change of heart and gave him an early parole.

As I've said before, I'm too nice, but the point is that I had won another huge moral victory for the ranch. Against tremendous odds, I had proved that there is no such thing as a Free-Throwed Tree Sloth. If you ever see a dull-witted creature walking around in a porcupine suit, it's a PORCUPINE.

And for your education on this matter, I've gone to the trouble to compose a little song on the subject of Thrills and Quills. Do we have time for you to listen to it? I guess so, sure. Here it is, and pay attention.

Thrills and Quills

If you see a short, fat beaver-tooth guy
   eating breakfast on a tree,
You'll probably think what most dogs

would, "He's only half as big as me."
And furthermore, you might observe how
   slow he moves around.
He waddles like a turtle, slow-motion on
   the ground.

And then you might check out his eyes to
   see how smart he looks:
Dumber than a box of rocks, he'd make the
   record books.
You put it all together and begin to see the
   light:
He's the one you've been waiting for to
   draw into a fight!

Never seek your thrills
From a guy who's wearing quills.
Bet you five you'll get your fill
Pretty quick, and you will.

But wait a second, you hear a voice
   whispering in your mind,
"I think I met this guy before, dark night,
   another time.
The details are a little hazy of that long ago
   report,
But it seems there might have been a fight,

and it was pretty short."

But caution doesn't fit a dog who's big,
    brave and strong.
If the other guy is dumb and slow,
    whatever could go wrong?
So you rush right into combat and jump the
    little jerk
And then it all comes back, he's wearing
    quills, and son, they hurt!

Never seek your thrills
From a guy who's wearing quills.
Bet you five you'll get your fill
Pretty quick, and you will.

Wow, is that an awesome song or what? No kidding, I mean, it's got action, adventure, and a very important moral lesson for dogs all over the world, and that's a pretty good day's work on this ranch.

This case is closed.

Have you read all of Hank's adventures?

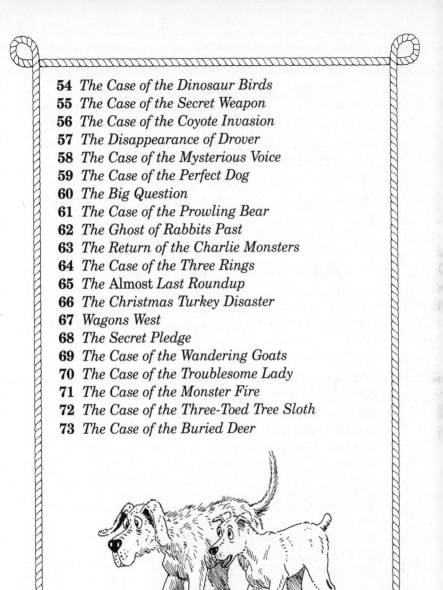

And, be sure to check out the
Audiobooks!

If you've never heard a *Hank the Cowdog* audiobook, you're missing out on a lot of fun! Each Hank book has also been recorded as an unabridged audiobook for the whole family to enjoy!

Praise for the Hank Audiobooks:

"It's about time the Lone Star State stopped hogging Hank the Cowdog, the hilarious adventure series about a crime solving ranch dog. Ostensibly for children, the audio renditions by author John R. Erickson are sure to build a cult following among adults as well." — *Parade Magazine*

"Full of regional humor . . . vocals are suitably poignant and ridiculous. A wonderful yarn." — *Booklist*

"For the detectin' and protectin' exploits of the canine Mike Hammer, hang Hank's name right up there with those of other anthropomorphic greats...But there's no sentimentality in Hank: he's just plain more rip-roaring fun than the others. Hank's misadventures as head of ranch security on a spread somewhere in the Texas Panhandle are marvelous situation comedy." — *School Library Journal*

"Knee-slapping funny and gets kids reading."

— *Fort Worth Star Telegram*

The following activities are samples from *The Hank Times*, the official newspaper of Hank's Security Force. Please do not write on these pages unless this is your book. And, even then, why not just find a scrap of paper?

"Rhyme Time"

W hat if Buzzy the Three-*Toed* Sloth decides to give up his life of loafing around and eating the trees on the ranch and go in search of other jobs? What kinds of jobs could he find?

Make a rhyme using "Woodrow" that would relate to his new job possibilities.

Example: **Toed** *repairs holes in socks and shirts?*
Answer: *Toed* **SEWED**

1. Toed starts a lawn care service.

2. Toed gets a job building highways.

3. Toed takes over for JT Cluck as Head Rooster.

4. Toed sells neon shirts.

5. Toes starts a gold mining company.

6. Toed makes lily pad rest-areas at ponds.

7. Toed gets packages into a truck and ready for delivery.

8. Toed gets a job as a speed bump.

Answers:

1. Toed MOWED
2. Toed ROAD
3. Toed CROWED
4. Toed GLOWED

5. Toed LODE
6. Toed TOAD
7. Toed LOAD
8. Toed SLOWED

"Photogenic" Memory Quiz

We all know that Hank has a "photogenic" memory—being aware of your surroundings is an important quality for a Head of Ranch Security. Now *you* can test your powers of observation.

How good is your memory? Look at the illustration on page 7 and try to remember as many things about it as possible. Then turn back to this page and see how many questions you can answer.

1. Who has the most feet on the ground? Hank, Drover, or Pete?

2. How many strands of barbed wire are there? 1, 2, 3, or 4?

3. Who has the highest tail? Hank, Drover, or Pete?

4. Which foot does Pete have at his mouth? Front Left, Front Left. or Back Left?

5. Who has the highest eye? Hank, Drover, or Pete?

6. How many of Drover's Eyes were visible? 1, 2 , 3, or all 4?

"Word Maker"

Try making up to twenty words from the letters in the names below. Use as many letters as possible, however, don't just add an "s" to a word you've already listed in order to have it count as another. Try to make up entirely new words for each line!

Then, count the total number of letters used in all of the words you made, and see how well you did using the Security Force Rankings below!

J T CLUCK ELSA

_____	_____
_____	_____
_____	_____
_____	_____
_____	_____
_____	_____
_____	_____
_____	_____
_____	_____
_____	_____

0 - 71 You spend too much time with J.T. Cluck and the chickens.

72 - 74 You are showing some real Security Force potential.

75 - 77 You have earned a spot on our Ranch Security team.

78 + Wow! You rank up there as a top-of-the-line cowdog.

Have you visited Hank's official website yet?

www.hankthecowdog.com

Don't miss out on exciting *Hank the Cowdog* games and activities, as well as up-to-date news about upcoming books in the series!

When you visit, you'll find:

- Hank's BLOG, which is the first place we announce upcoming books and new products!
- Hank's Official Shop, with tons of great *Hank the Cowdog* books, audiobooks, games, t-shirts, stuffed animals, mugs, bags, and more!
- Links to Hank's social media, whereby Hank sends out his "Cowdog Wisdom" to fans.
- A FREE, printable "Map of Hank's Ranch"!
- Hank's Music Page where you can listen to songs and even download FREE ringtones!
- A way to sign up for Hank's free email updates
- Sally May's "Ranch Roundup Recipes"!
- Printable & Colorable Greeting Cards for Holidays.
- Articles about Hank and author John R. Erickson in the news,

...AND MUCH, MUCH MORE!

BOOKS The Collection **FAN ZONE** Fun & Games **HANK THE COWDOG** **AUTHOR** Meet the Creator **STORE** Books & More

search the website GO

Find Toys, Games, Books & More
at the Hank shop.

ANNOUNCING: A sneak peek at Hank #66

Ever thought of having a Hank the Cowdog-Themed Party?

Hank Plays Cupid:

GAMES
COME PLAY WITH HANK & PALS

BOOKS
BROWSE THE ENTIRE HANK CATALOG

FRIENDS
GET TO KNOW THE RANCH GANG

Visit Hank's Facebook page

Follow Hank on Twitter

Watch Hank on YouTube

Follow Hank on Pinterest

Send Hank an Email

FROM THE BLOG

JAN 26 Hank is Cupid in Disguise...

JAN 18 The Valentine's Day Robbery! - a Snippet from the Story

DEC 04 Getting SIGNED Hank the Cowdog books for Christmas!

OCT 14 Education Association's lists of recommended books?

VISIT THE BLOG

Hank's Survey
We'd love to know what you think! GO

TEACHER'S CORNER
Download fun activity guides, discussion questions and more.

SALLY MAY'S RECIPES
Discover delicious recipes from Sally May herself. GO

Hank's Music.
Free ringtones, music and more!
MORE

Official Shop
Find books, audio, toys and more!
LET'S GO

Join Hank's Security Force
Get the activity letter and other cool stuff.
JOIN SECURITY FORCE

Get the Latest
Keep up with Hank's news and promotions by signing up for our e-news.
Looking for The Hank Times fan club newsletter?
Enter your email address SIGN UP

Hank in the News
Find out what the media is saying about Hank. GO

FEATURED BOOK

The Christmas Turkey Disaster
Now Available!
Hank is in real trouble this time. L...

BUY READ LISTEN

BOOKS
Browse Titles
Buy Books
Audio Samples
Other Books

FAN ZONE
Games
Hank & Friends
Security Force
Educational Stuff

AUTHOR
John Erickson's Bio
Hank in the News
In Concert
Contact John

SHOP
The Books
Store
Get Help

Love Hank's Hilarious Songs?

Hank the Cowdog's "Greatest Hits" albums bring together the music from the unabridged audiobooks you know and love! These wonderful collections of hilarious (and sometimes touching) songs are unmatched. Where else can you learn about coyote philosophy, buzzard lore, why your dog is protecting an old corncob, how bugs compare to hot dog buns, and much more!

And, be sure to visit Hank's "Music Page" on the official website to listen to some of the songs and download FREE Hank the Cowdog ringtones!

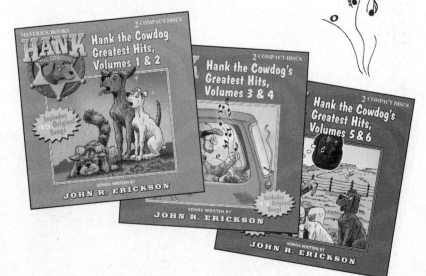

"Audio-Only" Stories

Ever wondered what those "Audio-Only" Stories in Hank's Official Store are all about?

The Audio-Only Stories are Hank the Cowdog adventures that have never been released as books. They are about half the length of a typical Hank book, and there are currently seven of them. They have run as serial stories in newspapers for years and are now available as audiobooks!

We all know Hank loves to eat ... and now *you* can try some of his favorite recipes!

Have you visited Sally May's Kitchen yet?

http://www.hankthecowdog.com/recipes

Here, you'll find recipes for:

Sally May's Apple Pie

Hank's Picante Sauce

Round-Up Green Beans

Little Alfred's and Baby Molly's Favorite Cookies

Cowboy Hamburgers with Gravy

Chicken-Ham Casserole

...and MORE!

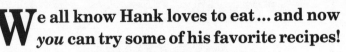

Teacher's Corner

Know a teacher who uses Hank in their classroom? You'll want to be sure they know about Hank's "Teacher's Corner"! Just click on the link on the homepage, and you'll find free teacher's aids, such as a printable map of Hank's ranch, a reading log, coloring pages, blog posts specifically for teachers and librarians, and much more!

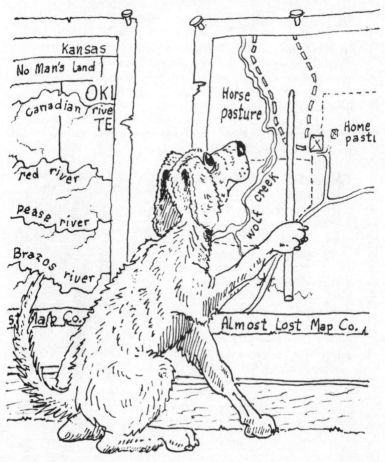

John R. Erickson,

a former cowboy, has written numerous books for both children and adults and is best known for his acclaimed *Hank the Cowdog* series. The *Hank* series began as a self-publishing venture in Erickson's garage in 1982 and has endured to become one of the nation's most popular series for children and families.

Through the eyes of Hank the Cowdog, a smelly, smart-aleck Head of Ranch Security, Erickson gives readers a glimpse into daily life on a cattle ranch in the West Texas Panhandle. His stories have won a number of awards, including the Audie, Oppenheimer, Wrangler, and Lamplighter Awards, and have been translated into Spanish, Danish, Farsi, and Chinese. *USA Today* calls the *Hank the Cowdog* books "the best family entertainment in years." Erickson lives and works on his ranch in Perryton, Texas, with his family.

Gerald L. Holmes

is a largely self-taught artist who grew up on a ranch in Oklahoma. For over thirty-five years, he has illustrated the *Hank the Cowdog* books and serial stories, as well as numerous other cartoons and textbooks, and his paintings have been featured in various galleries across the United States. He and his wife live in Perryton, Texas, where they raised their family, and where he continues to paint

his wonderfully funny and accurate portrayals of modern American ranch life to this day.